Also by Ariel Jade

Ravenous: Triskaidekaphilia Book 2

Psy-Brothers series (Coming soon!):
Alien Prince
Alien Captain
Alien Tamer

Alien Captain

Psy-Brothers #0.5

Ariel Jade

Seven Twenty-One Publishing
1231 Astra Ave.
Oshawa, ON
L1K 1H3
Canada
www.saboviec.com

Publisher's Note: This is a work of fiction. Names, characters, places, and incidents are a product of the author's imagination. Locales and public names are sometimes used for atmospheric purposes. Any resemblance to actual people, living or dead, or to businesses, companies, events, institutions, or locales is completely coincidental.

Alien Captain (Psy-Brothers #0.5) / Ariel Jade — 1st edition
ISBN 978-0-9952173-4-8

Chapter 1

Xaviara was mortified—from the top of her head to the bottom of her toes. She wished it was possible to sink into the floor of Sol Alliance Space Station 47, ooze into the engine room, and evaporate into tiny particles. That way, she wouldn't have to think about what a mess she'd gotten herself into.

"I can't believe the two of you." Manda, her boss, paced the floor in her small office in Sub-section Epsilon. "Childish antics like this."

Piotr stood next to her, arms easy at his sides. Xaviara wasn't a violent person, but she wanted to slap the smirk off his face. He thought this was *funny?* The only consolation was that Manda wheeled on him to thrust a finger into his face. He lifted a hand as though to ward her off, a tattoo of an infinity symbol surrounded by a circle visible on his wrist.

"Official reprimands in each of your files! Do you find *that* amusing?" she barked.

"She started it," said Piotr.

Xaviara bit her tongue, holding in a retort. She agreed with Manda. Their antics *were* childish, and to reply would be to underscore that fact. *He* was the one who'd started their rivalry when he'd joined the team, with his biting remarks about a project she'd been working on for weeks. He insulted her font choice, mocked the layout, and finished up with a doozy about lazy research. And was she supposed to take that? No. In retaliation, she'd been extra critical of his first project, and things spiraled out of control from there.

After several months, their disagreements had escalated—when *he* started actively trying to sabotage her. He'd been the one to hack into her account and steal her shower credits, a declaration, she'd decided, meant war.

But this latest...

"Do you think Gloria doesn't know that *you* planted the wrong video?" said Manda, finger still in Piotr's face. "You think she got to the rank of Senior Ambassador by being clueless to human behavior?"

He shrugged. The grin was slipping, at least.

Right in the middle of a presentation to the Senior Ambassador about an upcoming negotiation, Xaviara had inserted a video of the diplomatic team they were about to meet. However, smiling blue- and purple-skinned aliens completing their customary greeting was replaced with an embarrassing video of Xaviara dancing with—well, if she was being honest with herself, grinding on—some guy in one of the space station's clubs.

Piotr's smirk was now a scowl. "That wasn't me. Xaviara shouldn't have been given that responsibility. She made a mistake, and—"

"*That's enough.*" Manda sighed. "You embarrassed yourself in front of your boss's boss. *My* boss. This needs to stop and it needs to stop now."

Maybe she won't mention—

"And you! Dumping a cup of coffee in his lap!"

Heat flooded Xaviara's cheeks anew. She'd promised herself she wouldn't retaliate the next time he struck, that she would be the one to end it, but he was so smug. In a fit of rage, she'd lifted the lid of her coffee and thrown it into his lap. Xaviara had to admit that when his tablet got soaked and he knocked his own cup over, she felt vindicated.

Until his coffee sloshed across the table to soak Gloria's pristine, white suit.

"Piotr, go. I need to talk to Xaviara alone about the upcoming negotiations."

Piotr's face darkened even more, but he didn't argue. Xaviara couldn't help a strain of her own smugness rising inside.

"Official reprimands in both files!"

He scurried out, shoulders hunched.

When they were alone, Manda leaned against her desk. "Honestly, what has gotten into you? This isn't like you at all. You're usually my most reliable aide."

Xaviara looked at her hands. The small office felt cloistered, even with the Piotr gone. Sol Alliance Space Station 47 was a cozy home for Senior Ambassador Gloria Falchuk's diplomatic team—sufficient amenities for ambassadors and aides, although the truly opulent spaces were reserved for out-of-system guests. Today, it felt too small. Xaviara knew everyone and everyone knew her. And apparently, about this idiotic feud with Piotr.

"Do you need some time off?" prodded Manda.

"No!" said Xaviara. That would be a disaster. The entire rivalry centered around Piotr's desire to worm his way into Manda's good graces, although both had likely shattered whatever favorable opinion their boss had of them. Xaviara needed to prove Manda could count on her. "I'm fully prepared for the kadyyza's visit. Piotr just pushes my buttons."

"It's not— You don't have a crush?"

And Xaviara thought she couldn't become any more mortified. "He's gay, Manda. This isn't a schoolyard, pigtail-pulling thing."

"I know that. I wanted to make sure you did, too."

She was certain her face was brilliant red. "I'm not attracted to him." Definitely not. She couldn't see him as anything more than a thorn in her side—and an impediment to her career. Maybe it would be easier if she *did* find him attractive. Maybe then, she could set aside some of her fury.

"Fine. Then I'll tell you the same thing I told him. Find another outlet. Do something fun. Channel this urge to bicker into your recreation time. There are plenty of eligible men on this space station."

"I have a date tonight. A real one." One she was actually looking forward to. "He works security at the port." Which meant she didn't have to go through the awkward process of requesting permission. Members of the Sol Alliance Coalition had to register their romantic relationships. *What a way to kill whatever's budding.*

"That's good." Manda's voice softened. "I've been worried about you lately. Not just as a boss, but as a friend."

Xaviara waved a hand. Her career came first, which was why Piotr's sabotage upset her so much—not to mention her own reaction. She couldn't *not* respond, yet responding shot herself in the foot. "I have better things to do than get into something serious."

Manda squeezed her shoulder. "Regardless, I hope you have fun. Forget about Piotr. You don't have to prove anything to me. I know what a hard worker you are."

"You'll drop the reprimand then?" Xaviara dared to hope.

"I can't. Gloria insists. She wants to teach you two a lesson, and I have to say that in this instance, I agree with her. What if this had happened when the kadyyza were here? It would have been a diplomatic nightmare."

Xaviara slowly nodded. She hated the idea of a blemish on her record, but she could understand Manda's reasoning. "I'll be on my best behavior with the kadyyza. I promise."

"You'd better. You know how important this is to me." Earlier, Manda had shared in confidence that she was putting in for the position of Lead on this particular negotiation. Xaviara hoped she hadn't jeopardized that chance.

"Good luck." She was determined to keep to her word.

* * *

Xaviara, despite all attempts to convince herself otherwise, did not have a good time on her date. Tom was a good match on paper—steady if not glamorous job and full of witty anecdotes that were neither too short nor too lengthy.

And he was attractive, she supposed. Chiseled chest from the workouts he liked to brag about, dimples in both cheeks, tousled hair that always looked like he'd just rolled out of bed. But despite all that, the spark wasn't there.

In the interest of giving the poor man—and her libido—a chance, Xaviara accepted an invitation to return to his quarters for a nightcap, hoping a kiss or two would liven her up. But now she was alone in his small living space, considering how to gracefully make her exit, while Tom—such a staid, dull name—freshened up in his bathroom.

She tapped her fingers on the gray couch's armrest. That was the problem. Despite his initial charm, Tom was as boring as his name. *Curse you, brain.* Xaviara could never muster up attraction unless the man engaged her on an intellectual level. Oh, sure, he was full of stories, but they all had one thing in common. They took place here on the space station or in his home colony on Mars.

Xaviara hadn't trained as an international ambassador to settle down and raise children in the Sol System. She'd been patient as she went to university for four long years, and now that she was in her first year of a paid internship with a real diplomatic team, she wanted to get out of this place, see the galaxy.

Tom was taking a while in the bathroom. She glanced around the tiny quarters, contemplating. This apartment was the same footprint as hers as a first year aide. To seat more than two people at the slide-out dinner table, one had to shove the standard-issue couch against the wall. The colors Tom had chosen were boring gray, with hints of brown thrown in.

His empty inbox flashed on the wallscreen, devoid of even a flier for the upcoming holiday sale in the plaza's shopping center. As soon as they'd set foot in the apartment, he'd pressed a finger behind his ear to route his messages from his link—the implanted neural chip everyone had—over to the wallscreen.

That was another thing. Boring Tom had an unhealthy preoccupation with his link, something Xaviara detested. During the day, she was chained to hers, at the beck and call of her superiors. But unless they were in an active negotiation, the Sol Alliance Coalition had an ironclad rule around all employees taking sufficient downtime every day.

The inbox dinged, a nearly imperceptible sound that emanated from a small speaker at the base of the sofa. A symbol next to it indicated the message was encrypted, and it contained a blank subject and *No@Sender* in the From field.

This was the first intriguing thing she'd experienced about Tom.

Xaviara glanced toward the only inner door in the apartment. To the left was the bathroom. To the right was Tom's bedroom. It was probably the same drab gray as the sofa and wall trimming. She decided, in that moment, she would definitely never find out. *Sorry, self, guess the sex drought's gonna continue.* She was used to it, though. Despite the compromising video Piotr had taken of her, she didn't have the desire to take things any further than a dance. She longed for a real relationship—but not now. In the future. Once her career was sorted out.

In the bathroom, the water was running. Tom would be out any moment. But Xaviara had to find out why he'd been flicking his eyes to the right all night, the universal command to his link for *How many messages are waiting for me?*

Of course, it could be spam. All the technology in the world, and they'd still been unable to do away with unwanted advertisements.

Unable to convince herself, she reached out and swiped in the air to open the mail, a casual flick she told herself the computer could be mistaking for a command. *Oh, Tom, I sneezed and accidentally opened the message. You know how this interface is.*

It was short and full of additional characters that made it hard to read:

*^V@GK@L^ Preparations ^V@GK@L^ complete. ^V@GK@L^*

*^V@GK@L^ Operation Mallard ^V@GK@L^ Duck confirmed. ^V@GK@L^*

*^V@GK@L^ Negotiation team arrives ^V@GK@L^ tomorrow 22:00. ^V@GK@L^*

*^V@GK@L^ Attach previously provided packages to lead ship per ^V@GK@L^ schematics. Be prepared to receive further instructions. ^V@GK@L^*

*^V@GK@L^ First payment initiated ^V@GK@L^ to account on file. ^V@GK@L^*

Xaviara put a hand to her mouth. Part of her job as an aide was to know the docking schedule of all diplomatic teams. There was only one scheduled for tomorrow at 22:00 hours: the team of blue- and purple-skinned aliens, the kadyyza, for which Manda hoped to lead the negotiations. The aliens were to escort the humans—including Xaviara—back to their homeworld, simply called the First Planet, in the Imdali System, where they would finalize a treaty resolving contested mining rights, among other important provisions.

It was important. Exciting to be part of. And crucial to the human economy that it not fail.

"Packages" sounded ominous. What would be inside them? Surveillance equipments? A bomb?

She tipped her head to the left, wondering at the additional characters. Initials of some sort? De-encryption software failing to remove some of the embedded safety measures?

Tom was looking less boring than he had a few minutes ago, but Xaviara was loyal to her species, through and through. She had to do something—fast. She pressed a finger behind her ear to activate her link, blinked rapidly to take a snap of the wallscreen, and cycled through her contact list.

She flicked her wrist to close the interface as Tom came from the bathroom, his sexy smile now appearing sleazy. Whose payroll was he on? No matter. She needed to get out of here. It was possible he'd asked her out only because of her place on the ambassadorial team. She rose smoothly and took a step toward the door.

His face fell when he saw the inbox he'd left open—was he clueless or what?—and crossed the room in two strides to close it.

"Want something else to drink?" he asked.

They both looked at her glass. Only a few sips were gone from it. She used the movement to surreptitiously open a mail in her link. *Is my head swimming? Did he put something in that drink?* She quickly attached the snap she'd just taken, managed to type a few quick words behind her back, and flicked her eyes to initiate the send protocol.

Tom looked back at her. His brow furrowed—ugh, he wasn't so handsome that way, although maybe discovering that he was involved in something ugly made her distaste all the more potent. "Did you look at my mail?"

"No, of course not." Xaviara wanted to make her excuses and hightail it out of here, but she needed to keep him from destroying the evidence before the authorities could arrive. *They'll be here quickly, right?*

"That message showed as read." He was watching her, something lurking in his eyes.

She grasped at an explanation, her heart racing. "Oh, I just... I sneezed and—"

He stepped toward her. "You lying to me?"

She couldn't believe she'd found him handsome before. His face was twisted, his expression furious. Could she bolt out the door before he caught her? As part of her training, she took hand-to-hand combat lessons, but she'd never been in a real fight. Still, she could take him... even if he also practiced... Right?

As she poised to flee, the door beeped and slid open. A uniformed, masked man burst through, shouting something incoherent, followed by a second, third, fourth. "Hands where we can see them!" ordered the first.

Whoa, that was fast.

Tom leapt backward, face a shock of paleness. Xaviara put her hands in the air, but the masked men ignored her. They swarmed around her, yanking Tom's arms behind his back and securing him with electric cuffs before hustling him out the door. The leader turned to Xaviara, saluted, and said, "Miss." He hurried through the door and it slid shut behind him.

Xaviara was alone.

She exhaled, slowly lowering her arms.

Maybe Tom had more layers than she'd thought—not that it mattered anymore. She'd kept the delegation safe and gained brownie points with her management, plus the end of her date wasn't as boring as it could have been. She swaggered to the door, pleased with herself, and headed off to her own quarters.

She couldn't *wait* to rub Piotr's face in her discovery.

Chapter 2

"**N**o. Absolutely not. Under no circumstances." The Captain of the *Trincaar*'s Royal Guard, Nicholen, crossed his arms.

He stood with Camlan Valkkh in the tiny briefing room of the lead starship that would take them on a diplomatic mission to the human Sol System. The prince shifted his stance, and Nicholen matched him, centering his weight and resettling his arms. He tuned into his psy-sense—the ability all kadyyza possessed to read intense emotions—to scrutinize Camlan. Nicholen's particular ability manifested feelings as scents.

The *trincaar* was taller and more naturally muscled than Nicholen, but the smaller man knew he'd prevail in a wrestling match if Camlan instigated it, easily winning the argument. The table would get in their way, but if this was how he wanted to settle this, Nicholen trained six days a week in the gym, alternating weights with jogging and martial arts training.

But Camlan's eyes weren't sparkling, and Nicholen's psy-sense did not read the sugary mirth that went along with Camlan's jokes. This wasn't a teasing argument between now-adult men who'd been friends since they were children. The *trincaar* was serious.

"Those are your orders," said Camlan. He ran a hand over the deep indigo cape that marked his station as the *trincaarit*-in-waiting—king-in-waiting. Then he reached up to unhook it, and it cascaded from his shoulder to rest in the crook of his elbow.

"I can't impersonate you!" Nicholen took a deep breath and lowered his voice. Camlan was inured to his outbursts—the corner of his mouth quirked up. Nicholen would have a better chance of stopping this scheme if he kept calm and reasonable. "Besides, everyone will know who you are immediately. They'll see me. They'll know your Captain of the Guard is wearing the royal family's cape. Everyone knows what you look like. And then where will you be?"

"They won't. There are things you don't know about the royal family." The smile vanished. "There are things I didn't know about our genetic heritage until today. I have the ability to make people believe that they're looking at the *trincaar* when they look at you. Everything they know about me, all the audvids they've watched—you will replace me in their memory."

Nicholen's heart beat faster, as it did when he was preparing for an altercation. But this was not an enemy he could fight—and who was the enemy anyway? He didn't like not knowing something.

"Secrets make it impossible for me to do my job." It was the same thing he'd told Camlan three years ago, after he'd caught him sneaking out in the middle of the night to see some girl. That relationship hadn't lasted long anyway, and Nicholen would never understand why the prince put himself in such danger. But ever since the near-assassination that came as a result from Camlan's bad judgment, he was upfront with his lifelong friend and protector.

But Camlan only snorted. "Tell that to my father. He's the one with the secrets." He sighed. "Don't worry, I'm sure there's plenty more that *neither* of us know."

"Look, I feel for your father troubles," Nicholen really did, although Camlan wasn't making his relationship with the sovereign ruler of Imdali any easier, "but no. I refuse this order." As Captain, he was the only person who could override the prince's command. Even if they could pull it off, masquerading as Camlan would introduce too many risks in familiar territory, let alone on an alien space station light-years from home.

Camlan stood, back rigid, cape slung over one arm. Midnight eyes bored into Nicholen. "And I, too, am sorry. This is on order of the *trincaarit*. My father has asked—told us to do this."

Nicholen's mouth fell open. The *trincaarit* was the only person who could override his own order.

"Do I need to call him? Have him tell you directly?" Camlan asked.

Nicholen closed his mouth. He *hated* being undermined. "Get him in here."

Camlan pressed two fingers under his ear to activate his link. "Father? I told you he'd need more convincing."

Within a minute, the door swished open and the *trincaarit* strode inside. Nicholen inclined his head in a deep bow. The kadyyza people were programmed to be deferent to the royal family, a decision made by the geneticists who were the forebears to their entire species. The current geneticists had eased Nicholen's genetic commands for Camlan, but his instincts still kicked in full force with the appearance of the ruler of the entire Imdali System.

"Ah, Nicholen, my boy, good to see you again." Travid Valkkh gave a slight nod in acceptance to the captain's display of respect.

Nicholen fought against the desire to acquiesce. He was tasked with keeping the *trincaar* safe, and he couldn't do that while pretending to *be* the *trincaar*. "Your Excellency, I must strongly recommend against this course of action."

Camlan was a large man, but Travid was even larger. The similarities were striking; the older the son got, the more like his father he looked. Because Travid was the reigning ruler, Nicholen's psy-sense read nothing from him, another trait buried in kadyyza genetic code.

Travid said, "I'm not changing my mind. This must be done."

Nicholen had grown up in the royal household—his father was Captain of the *Trincaar*'s Royal Guard—but even so, it was difficult to think of arguing. Still, he managed, "Why?"

Even those midnight eyes were nearly identical. "Camlan has a lesson to learn."

The *trincaar* shuffled his feet. "Do we really need to—?"

"Let the man understand," said Travid. "My son has been having difficulty coping with Willex's death. Although it happened many years ago, he's been feeling unequal to the task of ruling as of late."

"Not exactly unequal—"

Travid silenced Camlan with a look. "You were never intended to rule. You stepped dutifully into the role, picking up the things you needed to learn, but you were just a boy at the time. Now, in your heart of hearts, you don't believe you can do it."

The eldest Valkkh brother had died in an accident when Camlan was a teenager. He was practicing off-roading in the forest, one of his favorite pastimes, when his vehicle hit a branch and tossed him into a swiftly moving river. He'd become entangled in a webbed shirt fashionable at the time and drowned before his security team managed to drag him out.

A full-scale, year-long investigation took place, but no charges were laid. Most of the family suspected that a terrorist organization called the *Geshhina Kadyyza* was involved, but every lead met a dead end. They were ruthless, bent on overthrowing the current government, and incredibly wily. Just the sort to evade detection.

Willex's death hit the entire family hard, but Nicholen had watched the weight of new responsibilities settle on Camlan's shoulders over the years. As of late, his long-time friend had been shirking duties, pissing off Travid's advisers, and making a spectacle of himself in "leaked" audvids on the neural net.

"How will my becoming *trincaar* help him with this?" Nicholen struggled to understand.

"He believes people only listen to him because of his title. He thinks he has nothing to offer as a person. I want him to use this opportunity to observe how people treat the *trincaar* and to make decisions on his own merit, as you do in the role of Captain of the Guard." Travid was still watching his son. "Are you able to complete this task?"

Nicholen's still didn't like it, but the reasoning seemed somewhat solid. "I'll do whatever you need. It's just..." He trailed off. How could he explain? Because he'd grown up in the royal household, his position as captain for one of the princes seemed guaranteed. But he didn't want to be *handed* the position. He needed to earn it—every single day he was on the job. "The *trincaar*'s safety will be at risk if I'm not operating with my own authority."

"You'll have *his* authority," said Travid.

Nicholen frowned. How could he argue with that? Besides, his resolve was crumbling as the genetic predisposition took over, making him want to ask forgiveness from his sovereign leader. He was too proud for that, but, "Fine." He turned to his prince and long-time friend. "Just don't do anything stupid."

The corner of Travid's mouth lifted in a small smile. He knew his son as well as Nicholen did.

"Of course I won't." Camlan's grin was back, the one that lit up the neural net audvids and kept half the solar system obsessing over his relationship status on social media.

Nicholen might not be able to influence Travid, but he definitely could influence Camlan. "I'm serious. *That* is an order."

"Yes, sir." Camlan mock-saluted, and Nicholen's psy-sense picked up his mood again—sugary-sweet and teasing. Nothing ever got him down, that was for sure.

Travid plucked Camlan's cape from the crook of his elbow. "Here. You'll need to wear this to pass as royalty. You must act as similarly to Camlan as possible."

"If I may," Nicholen had difficulty getting the words out, but he needed to know, "how does this work?"

Travid looped the cape around Nicholen's shoulders. "The forebears buried secrets in our DNA. The royalty's psy-abilities are much greater than is commonly known. I tell you at great risk—it is important this information does not leave this room. But I trust you with my son's life, so I must trust you with this."

The cape settled around Nicholen's shoulders, and the reality of what the *trincaarit* was ordering sunk in. *Nicholen* would be acting as *trincaar*, greeting the human delegation, pretending to be something he was not. Sure, he'd grown up watching the Valkkh brothers learn how to be princes, but acting one himself was completely different.

"You'll do fine. I know it." Travid's hand was heavy on his shoulder.

Chapter 3

The next morning, Xaviara hurried to the office sub-section, hoping for praise from her boss for thwarting whatever sabotage was afoot. Instead, Manda was in a tizzy over preparations.

"Gloria agreed that I could be Lead on this negotiation," she said. "We have to be ready to receive them."

"Er," said Xaviara, "what about—"

"They're arriving this afternoon and I'm not even remotely prepared. Can you take notes?"

Xaviara pulled out her tablet, annoyed. She was hoping for kudos after the embarrassing incident with Piotr. "Yes."

Manda plucked a tablet off a desk covered in a haphazard array of several. "I really need to consolidate these, don't I? What am I saying? There's not time for that. We have to get ready for the kadyyza."

The treaty with the kadyyza was important for two reasons: both economies would benefit from increased trade, and it would put to rest a long-standing hostility that had cropped up over rights to mine particles from a space anomaly. Over a decade ago, the animosity reached a fevered pitch when the rivalry spiraled out of control into a full-on battle. Several hundred civilian human and kadyyza space miners died that day, referred to as the Day of Darkness.

As a result, both sides finally realized it was time to do something to mend relations between themselves. An interim treaty had been put into place, and both species' governments pushed goodwill ads to the populace for years. This treaty was the final step in solidifying relations, so Manda's nervousness was understandable.

"I think their quarters are ready," said Manda, "but I want to check one more time. Plus the reception room! We have to make sure their flag is hung properly. We don't want an incident like when I was an aide, when a coworker accidentally hung a flag upside down. Did you know that's why relations with the mymni are strained?"

"I didn't."

"Also, don't forget how to say their names if you have the occasion—surname, then given. Valkkh Camlan, for instance."

"Yes, Manda." Listening, agreeing—those were the things that would get on Manda's good side. But Xaviara couldn't stand it anymore. She blurted, "What happened to Tom?"

Manda looked up from her tablet. "Tom?"

"The guy from last night? The one I caught with the suspicious mail?"

"Oh." Manda looked back down. "I turned it over to Coalition security. Did they arrest him?"

"Yeah, about three seconds after I sent the mail. They busted in and hustled him out."

"Wow." The stream of words had been momentarily staunched. "They really move, don't they?"

"I guess so. What about the sabotage?"

"What about it?" Manda swiped rapidly through kadyyza dossiers.

"Shouldn't we be worried about it?"

"No, I'm sure they've got it under control. We have other things to do."

"But what if—"

"Never mind!" Manda stopped swiping. "I'm sorry. That was uncalled for. Honestly, in all the years I've been with the Coalition, we've never had a problem with security. If a plot was afoot to sabotage the negotiation, they've squashed it like a bug. Promise."

Xaviara wasn't convinced. "Is someone from the security team coming with us to Imdali?"

"If they think it's necessary, they will." Manda went back to swiping. She stopped on a picture of the *trincaar*. "The prince sure is handsome, isn't he?" She gasped, face reddening. "Sorry. I guess I hadn't noticed before. This picture... It does him justice."

"It does." Xaviara glanced down at the dossier. Prince Camlan definitely was attractive, with his indigo skin, a perfect mix between the various colors of their species.

But the man who caught her eye was his Captain of the Royal Guard, Nicholen. He had a rougher look to him— more military, with short cropped hair and a glint in his eye that made her stomach flip.

"But never mind all that." Manda closed the dossiers. "We have more important things to worry about than men, don't we?"

"Yes, we do."

"All right, so as I was saying about the flag. Can you see to it personally?"

* * *

Xaviara spent the day checking off items on Manda's list, along with the other three aides, Rosa, Kristoph, and her rival, Piotr. That afternoon, Manda jittered in the reception room, side-eying her aides for the tenth time.

"Fix your collar, Kristoph," she said. "I've asked three times."

Xaviara's co-aide looked down at his shirt, shrugged, and smoothed a hand over it.

"Let me just do it myself!" Manda stalked across the room, popped the collar up and out, and then laid it back down.

The door opened. The four aides and the now-Lead, Manda, snapped into a straight line.

The blue-skinned alien who walked through the door first was short and muscular. Xaviara blinked as the room went watery, slid to the side, and then righted itself. Dizzy, she managed to hold in a gasp, although Manda gave her a sharp look. Xaviara blinked rapidly, accidentally taking a snap of the entourage.

Manda stepped forward to complete introductions while Xaviara held in a breath and waited for whatever sickness this was to pass. *Now is not the time for food poisoning.* But it wasn't nausea. It was something else, a disorientation she'd never felt before. Finally certain she wasn't going to fall over, she let out a breath and studied the group.

What she realized almost made her gasp again.

The *trincaar* was there, all right, but he was skulking in the back, while Captain of the Guard Nicholen wore the deep indigo cape and acted in the role Camlan should have.

What in the blazes is going on? Xaviara was *certain* the dossiers had shown something different. Camlan's classically handsome face had stared back from the file marked *Imdali System Trincaar*, and Nicholen's had glared from the file marked *Imdali System Captain of the* Trincaar *'s Guard.* And she'd seen audvids of the playboy prince in action! Partying, winking at the camera... But they'd switched positions.

Stranger still was that no one seemed fazed except Xaviara.

Completing the kadyyza greeting perfectly, Manda kissed her fingers and held them to the faux prince with the air of diplomatic politeness. None of the other aides look as confused or uncomfortable as Xaviara felt. Piotr and Rosa were both staring raptly at Nicholen, the fake prince, whose shoulders were rigid and movements stiff.

Should she say something? Why this ruse?

Part of Xaviara's research for Manda had been into the special abilities the kadyyza possessed, besides the species' psychic ability to sense emotion. A civil war had nearly wiped them out centuries ago, and as part of the truce, the leaders had genetically engineered the royal line to rule in fairness and justice for all, with an inborn loyalty to their people so deeply ingrained in their genes that it could never be broken.

Whatever the *trincaar* was doing, he believed he was doing it for the good of his people.

Far be it from me to unveil their little charade, decided Xaviara. After all, secrets were the trade of ambassadors, and it looked like she possessed one her human delegation knew nothing about. It might come in handy somewhere between the human solar system and the kadyyza one.

Satisfied, she looked up to see the fake prince's bright, violet eyes boring into hers.

This time, she almost staggered at the weight of the muscular, handsome man giving her a searing once-over. *He's the real captain*, she told herself. *He's just checking to ensure you're not a threat.*

But Xaviara's heart fluttered faster when he held her gaze.

My, but he was well-built. She'd found him attractive when looking through the dossiers before—everyone fawned over the *trincaar*, but Xaviara preferred her men a little dangerous. Camlan seemed goofy, whereas Nicholen seemed the *real* backbone of this entire delegation. He was short but powerful, and despite his obvious discomfort, he moved with the grace of a predator. Beneath the official uniform of the royal family were muscles she could see herself falling asleep on.

What am I thinking? But she couldn't look away from those brilliant violet eyes, as desire buzzed inside her. His stare penetrated her soul, and she bit her lip to keep from letting out a squeak. When he tore his gaze from her and settled it on Manda, she nearly sighed at the loss.

Oh, yes. For more reason than one, this was going to be an interesting few days.

* * *

The moment Nicholen stepped into the reception room, three things struck him.

First, the humans were impeccable in their diplomacy. He'd accompanied Camlan on these delegations off and on his whole life, and he'd never seen a single group so well-organized as this one seemed to be.

Second, he did *not* like the spotlight. Kissing the fingers of the Lead was a hell of an awkward thing for him, and he was certain Manda Aurellia was going to call him out any second. He almost regretted that she didn't—at least then, this terrible ordeal would be over instead of only beginning.

And third, the aide in the back with the long, black hair who seemed distracted by something—the only break in protocol—was the most beautiful woman he'd ever seen.

As if he didn't have enough to concern himself with, he couldn't keep his eyes from her face. She seemed young and sweet, but her eyes held an intelligence unmatched by any other person—kadyyza, human, or other—that he'd ever met. Manda, the Lead, was clearly a bright woman, or she wouldn't have been given this important assignment so early in her career. But this aide, Xaviara—he rolled the name over in his mind; it reminded him of a beautiful winged insect in their home system—possessed a self-awareness that bored into him.

He chanced another look over at her. She was staring. When he met her deep, brown eyes, something sparked through him to settle in his groin. He nearly let out a moan.

These were absolutely the wrong thoughts to be having at a time like this. He would need to stay far away from her if he was to concentrate on the task at hand. Nicholen quickly looked back to the Lead, who'd been going through the customary greetings with the rest of the kadyyza.

"May we show you around the space station?" asked Manda.

Nicholen realized half a beat too late she was talking to him—the fake *trincaar*. "Please. We'd be delighted." *Ugh, I'm doing fucking terrible here.* They'd think him slow, a poor representation of Camlan, if he kept this up. He didn't agree with the *trincaarit*'s orders, but he would do as he was told. He'd better get his shit together.

But those eyes... That hair... Her straight posture and coy smile.

Involuntarily, he shuddered, covering it with a gesture to smooth over the hated indigo cape.

Focus, Nicholen. You career is at stake here.

Chapter 4

Nicholen had no time to ponder what the searing eye contact with the beautiful aide meant. The human Lead seemed determined to leave the space station as soon as possible, a decision he didn't agree with. A magnetic storm was brewing in mu-space, and as Captain, he would have much preferred to wait out the storm. As prince, he had to balance his own opinions with diplomacy.

Fucking diplomacy. There was a reason he preferred his job. "Shoot first, ask questions later" had served him well.

At 08:00 hours the next morning, the delegation gathered to discuss. He and Camlan sat on one side of the table, and Manda sat on the other next to a woman named Gloria, who was the Senior Ambassador on the team. He was unclear on why Gloria wasn't leading the delegation, but he chalked it up to another species's quirk.

"Why chance it?" asked Nicholen.

"I've told you why," said Manda.

"No, that's not what I meant. I meant what's the harm in waiting another month?"

"Would you like me to bring up the chart again?"

Manda had, of all things, a multi-colored chart showing timelines and lost revenues, all of which made Nicholen's head spin. Numbers were not his forte.

"I'm not asking about harm to the economy but to your diplomatic team." Maybe he could wheedle her into a corner, make her admit to something untoward. "What promises have you made to your higher-ups?"

Senior Ambassador Gloria was frowning now, and Camlan cleared his throat. "Gloria, have *you* had a chance to review Manda's navigation route? I looked at it last night, and I found are several pockets of magnetic winds that might throw us off course."

"I have. And I defer to Manda's judgment. She's Lead on this mission."

And now they were back to where they'd started. Nicholen was growing more and more frustrated.

"Gentlemen." Manda's tone sounded like the dismissive one Nicholen used during interrogations. "We have matters to attend to. The decision has been made, the crew informed. If there's nothing else, we need to prepare for our departure."

"Gloria," said Camlan, thankfully, as Nicholen was about to lose his temper, "you're the ranking official in your department. Is there a reason you're letting Manda move forward with such a reckless plan?"

Rather than answering, Gloria looked at Manda, and Manda looked at Nicholen. "*Trincaar*, I suggest you bring your captain under control. If you do not, I will have no choice but to file a grievance with the Unified Federation of Solar Systems."

Oh, by the forebears, give me a fucking break. This woman was grating on every last one of his nerves, and he had no idea what the *real* prince of Imdali would say in this situation. He'd probably find it amusing but demand an apology just the same. "Camlan?" Nicholen tried to sound stern.

"I'm sorry, Ambassadors. I spoke out of turn. If required, the *trincaar* will have my resignation in hand before we depart tomorrow."

Now he's just playing games. Nicholen hated this ruse already.

"That won't be necessary, Captain."

Camlan bowed his head in the most ridiculous display of mock deference Nicholen had ever seen. From that alone, he expected the human ambassadors to know something was amiss.

But instead, Manda stood. "Now then. Thank you for bringing your concerns to my attention. I will see you at noon for takeoff."

* * *

The only good thing about leaving so soon was that they didn't have to stay at the human space station long. The shorter the trip, the sooner Nicholen could get back to being Captain of the Guard.

Despite Manda watching them like a hawk—something she didn't even attempt to disguise—Nicholen managed safety checks of the starships. As part of the diplomatic protocol, two ships would make their way to Imdali. The first was the lead ship, manned only by the Captain of the Guard and the Lead. The second was the anchor ship, with the rest of the humans and kadyyza.

The idea of the real *trincaar* being on the lead ship sent Nicholen into a near-frenzy. The whole concept of a lead ship was a leftover tradition from the early days of kadyyza spacefaring. He decided to talk to Camlan about it.

"We're going to tell the humans we've decided the prince will be on the lead ship. It's more logical anyway," he started.

Camlan laughed, and his mischievous attitude brushed Nicholen's psy-sense with sweetness. "Nope."

"I can't let you be alone on a lead ship. You're much safer here, surrounded by my guards." Couldn't Camlan see that?

"We promised my father we would do this." His jaw was set in a way that said he wasn't budging. "Besides, what's the worst that can happen?"

Right. Because nothing bad ever came after those words. "But I'm the *real* head of security. *I'm* supposed to be on that ship."

"How long do you want to fight about this?" said Camlan.

"Do we even need a lead ship? Maybe we could forgo it this time."

"I'm the protector of our customs as much as you're the protector of me."

"That's not what you tell your father all the time!"

"Oh, I just like to shake things up a bit. When it's an important tradition, I make sure it gets done." Camlan's eyes took on a faraway look. "Besides, I don't think Manda would stand for that."

Nicholen's mouth fell open. "Are you *smitten* with her?"

"No!" Camlan's face was flushing from its usual indigo to a deep purple.

"You *are*. By the forebears, Camlan, *be fucking careful.*"

"That's enough. I'm still your prince, and I'm not going to have a conversation about my love life *again*. Who I date is my business."

"So you want to date her?"

"Enough." Camlan drew himself to his full height. Not a trace of sugar now, only steel. "Go do one more safety check. I'll ensure she's distracted."

And that was that. It made Nicholen growly. Extremely growly.

Takeoff happened without a hitch, but once in muspace, Nicholen paced around the anchor ship relentlessly. It was large enough to accommodate two dozen humanoids, yet he felt like a *fuvvia* trapped in its stall. The ship was only mid-range, which meant no exercise facilities. *What I wouldn't give for a punching bag.*

Three hours after liftoff, they were deep in remote territory. This long stretch between the Sol System and the

Imdali System wasn't precisely uncharted, but it was no longer settled. Long-abandoned terraforming projects abounded out here, from the centuries ago when many species were expanding. Due to the length of time it took to travel, the projects had sucked up precious money and resources. The galaxy was in a recession, with most species focusing their energy on the planets, moons, and asteroids within their home systems.

Traveling through it made him nervous.

He was marching around the corner, trying and failing not to fret, when he knocked into the long-haired aide from the reception room. The contact was over in a second, but she was so *soft*. Sparks shivered down his spine, and his manhood stirred as he realized he'd brushed her breast.

She gasped and blushed. "H-hello... *trincaar*." She kissed her fingers and held them out for the traditional kadyyza greeting.

Nicholen's heart pumped faster at the impressive display of manners. Even the minor aides were schooled in their ways. He took great pleasure in grasping her small hand in his and bringing it to his lips. When he kissed the tip of her middle finger, something new thrilled through him, something primal and protective. She was diminutive but fierce, as had been evidenced by the way he'd seen her ordering the other aides around. "Good day to you."

"My name is Xaviara." Again, that gorgeous name, just like the *viaar* on his homeworld, a winged insect he supposed was akin to Earth's butterflies. "I hope all is well with the, ah, captain and my boss?"

"Oh, yes." The way she'd said that was odd, but she was flushing a pretty pink, and he couldn't stay on that line of thought for long. "You seem to enjoy working with the ambassadors."

"I do! I've always wanted to be a part of diplomatic relations between humans and other races, ever since I was a little girl." And now she was glowing. Her enthusiasm was enchanting. He could have listened to it all day.

"A woman who knows what she wants. I like it." Nicholen could relate. Security for the royal family was a highly coveted position, and he'd wanted this position since he was a boy.

Xaviara was flushing again, and her scent was slightly floral—alluring. It was so subtle, Nicholen wasn't sure if it was his sense of smell picking up on a shampoo or his psy-sense signaling a subtle emotion. What would it be like to pull her into a side room, take out some of his frustrations in a better way than storming around the ship? From the way she was looking up at him from under her eyelashes, she *might* be thinking the same thing.

When was the last time he'd let his fantasies get away from him like this? He was being ridiculous now.

"All seems to be going well." Xaviara held her poise admirably, which made him want to bite that bottom lip all the more. "I just came from the bridge."

He inclined his head. "Yes."

"It's just that you seem... worried." She tipped her head back, looked up at him.

She seemed so open, so inviting. He wished he could confess his troubles to *someone*. He had no real companions, especially not within the delegation. He grasped at something to say to keep her talking to him longer.

A klaxon blared. She startled.

"What the fuck?" he swore under his breath.

Xaviara's brown eyes were wide. "Do you think the... Are they... ?"

"I don't know but we'd better find out."

"Warning," droned the ship's AI, "lead ship for delegation KH-159 off course. All personnel, rendezvous on the bridge."

This time, Nicholen's string of epithets were colorful metaphors that likely went completely over his human companion's head, if her translator was able to keep up at all. He turned on his heel and marched toward the bridge, not even worrying that he was falling back to movements that seemed too crisp or military for a prince. This ridiculous charade would have to wait.

His *trincaar* was in trouble, and he had no time to waste in finding out what was happening.

Chapter 5

Xaviara had no reason to be on the bridge, no official function in a crisis like this, but she scuttled in after Nicholen and tried to blend into the wall. She had to know what was happening to Manda and the real prince; a second-hand account after a nail-biting wait wouldn't do.

The bridge was a chaos of blaring computer warnings and crew hunched over consoles. The navigation officer manually piloted their ship's controls, and the communication officer repeated a message over and over. "Lead ship KH-159, come in, please. Advise your status. This is anchor ship KH-159. Please come in."

The front wallscreen displayed a stunning blue and green planet with swirling clouds—like Earth but with more vibrant colors. They were no longer in mu-space. Instead, they were stopped in a solar system halfway between Sol and Imdali.

"What's happening?" demanded Nicholen, indigo cape flying behind him as he stormed up to the navigation officer, Anthony.

"They must have hit a pocket in the magnetic storm. They've been knocked out of mu-space, and they're spinning out of control." Anthony's fingers tweaked tri-D controls in front of the console. *He must be settling us into orbit.*

"There has to be something we can do." Nicholen leaned over the console, corded muscles rippling. "Turn on a tractor beam! Pull them out of there!"

"They're caught in the gravity well of that planet." Anthony seemed to be visibly steeling himself not to cower. "The tractor beam would do no good."

"How could this have possibly happened?" Nicholen turned heel again—a crisp movement that was no doubt courtesy of his military background, a fact no one but Xaviara seemed to have noticed yet. She loved watching him. He was so efficient, so *intense.* "I went over the flight plans myself, and the magnetic storm should be nowhere near us."

No one questioned why the *trincaar* would be reviewing flight plans. Anthony was focused on the controls, and the communication officer droned the message. Nicholen punched buttons on the console, zooming in on the lead ship. It was spinning on its horizontal axis—not wildly out of control, but Xaviara had no idea how they were going to stabilize it with the speed it had picked up.

Goosebumps prickled up her arm. *Poor Manda.* Xaviara had never received very good marks in her flight classes, but she knew what an out-of-control object looked like.

Gloria appeared at the door. The black woman's eyes swept across the room and landed on the kadyyza "prince." "Calm yourself, Nicholen. My staff is doing the best they can."

He wheeled on her, violet eyes sparking. "Is that so? You do realize that our people are—"

A siren blared again, and the AI coolly informed the chaotic room, "Lead ship KH-159 is now on a collision course for planet UTP-8907."

"*For all the crimson-shaded leaves in the—*" Xaviara's translator failed at whatever word Nicholen shouted next.

"*Trincaar.*" Gloria glided into the room. Though she was tall and thin, her presence demanded the attention of everyone. "Manda Aurellia is the best pilot that I have ever known. If anyone can land them safely on the planet, she can. And as I understand it, your captain has also won awards for his flying."

Nicholen bit his lip so hard blood welled.

Nicholen is the one with the awards. The trincaar *is only...* Well, Camlan was known as a good flier, too, but she could see the way Nicholen was glaring at the wallscreen. He must be thinking he should be the one in the downward spiral toward the planet now. His protective instincts made something inside Xaviara flare. What would it be like to have him care that much about *her?*

The ship was lost under a covering of clouds now. When it reappeared, it was tiny. Nicholen attempted to magnify it, but the picture went grainy. It was difficult to tell if the ship was still spinning.

They have to get it under control, or they won't survive the crash.

As if in response, the AI said, "Lead ship KH-159 stabilized landing trajectory. Landing zone predicted at 43.916 latitude, -78.924 longitude."

"Now, see," said Gloria. "They're going to be fine."

The bridge was silent except for a staccato beep. They watched on the screen as the ship disappeared again under a cloud. The room seemed to hold its breath. Anthony swiped to pull up a rendering of what was happening, using information pulled from the lead ship's sensors: a black background with a cartoon-like white ship and ground.

"Lead ship KH-159 losing altitude," said the AI. "Lead ship KH-159 on target for landing zone. Lead ship KH-159 losing altitude."

The ship came close to the ground, landed, bounced once, and landed again.

As it finally came to a rest, Nicholen let out a long breath. "They're stuck on that planet until we figure out a way to get them off."

"Of course," Gloria said.

"This ship is too big to land on an object that large. It was never meant for anything except docking at space stations."

"I know that."

"And—"

The AI cut him off. "Communications lost with lead ship KH-159. Strong magnetic fields of planet UTP-8907 are interfering with uplink. Please stand by. Please stand by. Please stand—"

"Turn that thing off!" shouted Nicholen, as the communication officer cut the voice.

"*Trincaar.*" Gloria's voice was smooth but steely. "I would suggest a breather. *We* will handle this situation and get your man off the planet safely."

"But I—"

"No one was ever saved by anyone whose emotions were raging out of control."

Xaviara was offended on his behalf. He was taking charge of the situation, protecting his prince. It was his *job*. But, of course, no one else knew that.

Nicholen's face was dark blue. "The lead ship only has emergency supplies for two weeks. We can't waste any time mounting a rescue."

"I agree, and I assure you, we *will* rescue him," finished Gloria. "You know as well as I how important this delegation is to humans."

"Let me—"

"Not right now." Gloria could be cold when she wanted to be. This woman got what she wanted.

Nicholen opened his mouth.

"This is *our* responsibility. Don't make me order you off the bridge." It was a ballsy statement, but given that humans were the lead party in this diplomatic delegation, Gloria would do it. The words were spoken quietly—a Senior Ambassador to an unruly prince.

Xaviara prickled. This was the same woman who'd insisted on the official reprimand because of she and Piotr's pranks. Gloria was unforgiving, and Xaviara decided she absolutely didn't like her.

Nicholen pressed his lips together, and they turned an even darker shade of blue than usual. "Fine." Once more, his turn was crisp, the snap of his cape more practiced than it was the day they arrived.

He stalked off the bridge.

She really shouldn't go after him, but his attractiveness was getting the better of her. Romantic relations between diplomatic teams were strictly forbidden until the treaty was signed because of the possible influence on the negotiations. She could lose her job and any prospect of being a full ambassador someday.

But he needed help—he would be floundering now that he was kicked off the bridge—and she couldn't just let him wallow in the unknown, worrying about his prince alone.

Besides, she could resist him. And who was to say he was attracted to her in return? He was much too distracted to consider anything bu saving Camlan right now.

The crew, including Gloria, turned to the wallscreen, now covered with streams of data.

Unnoticed, Xaviara hurried off after him.

* * *

Nicholen glared humans and kadyyza out of the way as he stormed toward his quarters.

This was an absolute, full-on, unmitigated disaster. It overshadowed the near-assassination of several years ago like a gas giant over one of its moon. As soon as they got Camlan out of this mess—and they *would* get Camlan out of this mess—he was going to give *everyone* a piece of his mind. The *trincaar*, the head of security for the royal family, the *trincaarit* himself—despite his genetic predisposition.

He punched the button on his room, and the door slid open with hardly a sound, plunging him into an even fouler mood. When they were on the homeworld, at least he could slam doors with verve and vigor and have them respond in kind.

As he stepped inside, someone caught his eye. Xaviara hovered at the far end of the corridor, looking like she was unsure whether to approach cautiously or flee in terror. He stopped halfway through and growled, "What is it?"

She twirled to look behind herself, hair fanning out.

"Yes, you, what is it? You followed me from the bridge. You might as well come over here and tell me what you want."

Seeing the sexy aide made some of his frustration melt away, much to his dismay. He needed to be focusing on getting Camlan off the planet—but Senior Ambassador Gloria had mowed over all his protestations and never looked back.

Xaviara came down the hallway, looking for all the galaxy like she was going to bolt at any moment.

"I won't bite." He forced a smile. "Not unless you want me to, that is."

She blushed again—forebears, he loved that shade. He moved out of the way to allowed her into his quarters, which were little more than a cell with a bed and a small writing table. And this was the opulent suite for the *trin-caar*—these ships were not made for long-range travel. The two days between their systems was pushing its limits. She stepped inside, the door slid shut behind her, and he suddenly realized they were alone in the cramped space.

"Do you want to go to the mess hall?" It wasn't an enormous improvement, but at least others would be around.

"This is fine. Actually, I have something I need to say, and it's best if we're alone."

Every fiber of his being hummed with the desire to know what she could possibly have to say to him alone. He pointed to the desk chair bolted to the floor.

She shook her head. "I don't even know where to start with this."

"At the beginning?" His blood was still pumping quickly, but no longer from the earlier fury. She was so curvy, so small, so perfect, even in the mole that graced her cheek.

She stared at her fingernails and then blurted, "I think someone sabotaged the lead ship."

"*What?*" he roared.

She shuddered but didn't cringe back. "I didn't tell you sooner because... Well..."

Out came the story of her botched date—a fact that relieved him enormously, since that meant she was single. *Focus, man*, he admonished himself. Then she explained about the mail and Manda's subsequent dismissal of her concerns. She forwarded him the snap of the mail, with the cryptic letters embedded within. He studied it and then returned to her story. When she got to the end, he'd reined in his fury enough that he stood seething in silence, wishing he could pace again.

"I know it doesn't matter who did it, not exactly," she said, "but I'm afraid this might only be the beginning. It could be anyone, and they're probably on our ship right now."

"Yes. This is concerning." His mind raced, going over the possibilities. Was it kadyyza? Was it human? It could be anyone—the delegates Camlan had brought or even Gloria herself. He eyed the short woman in front of him, trying and failing not to note her well-rounded curves. *Xaviara wouldn't tell me this if she were the saboteur, would she?*

"That's not all." She seemed to be forcing out the words.

"Of course it's not." *Storms don't travel alone*—an old kadyyza proverb. "Go on."

"Um... You see... I don't know how you did it, but whatever you did didn't work on me."

The words were rushed, and Nicholen couldn't figure out what she was saying. Was the translator failing? "What do you mean? Slow down."

She blew out a breath. "I know why you're so upset. I know you're not the *trincaar*. Whatever you or Camlan did, it didn't work on me. I know the real prince is stuck down on the planet."

Without thinking, Nicholen swept the knife from his ankle holster, pushed Xaviara against the wall, and held it at her throat.

Chapter 6

One minute, Xaviara's body was aflame with the close proximity to this muscled dream in his tiny quarters—and she could get in *so* much trouble for being alone with him. The next, he was pressed up against her with her back to the wall and a knife hovering near her throat. She swallowed and said, "Nicholen, if I'd wanted to harm to you or your prince, would I have told you I know your secret?"

The knife wasn't touching her, but his entire torso was against hers and his lips were mere inches away. She was relieved to note that he wasn't aroused by this display of machismo—only, perhaps, resigned, by the hard set of his jaw—but she wasn't in the same boat. Something about his stance and the way he held the knife told her this was all bravado, or maybe even an automatic reaction to show his command of the situation, fueled by years of training.

She lifted a hand and gently placed it on the knife. "You need my help. The saboteur could be anyone. And I'm the only one who knows how dire the situation is. Unless you want to announce to all the humans that your prince is stuck on a wild planet. I assume all the kadyyza already know?"

His intake of breath told her they did.

She pulled the knife from his grasp and tossed it aside. It clunked onto the desk, coming to rest on the console open to a screen more fit for a captain of the guard than a *trincaar*. If she'd had any doubts about his true identity, they were washed away with the symbol displayed in the upper corner, the official seal of the Imdali Royal Guard.

His head moved almost imperceptibly in a nod. Without the knife, they were just two people alone in a room, bodies pressed together, attraction sizzling between them. The forbidden fraternization made the captain all the more delicious. Her nipples bloomed as she realized the shifting movement at her waist was a clear sign that he was responding to her closeness. She held still, though she longed to press herself against his erection and see how far she could take this.

But they had bigger things to worry about.

She licked her lips. "We need to start an investigation. Find out who it is." *When is he going to pull away?* she wondered at the same time her entire body screamed, *No, stay.* Kadyyza body temperature was warmer than human, and his proximity was heating her up in more ways than one.

He cleared his throat, his eyes roving over her face like he was trying to drink in her features. "We need to stop whatever plan they have." His half-erection shifted against her leg.

"Yes, I agree, but..." Her hand was drifting toward his torso. If he kissed her, she wouldn't be able to hold back. "... we can only stop what they're doing when we know who they are."

He blinked and pulled back. "Sorry... I'm sorry... I didn't mean to..." And then, sadly, his warmth—and man-hood—were gone. "It was just..."

"I get it," she said. He was so protective of the prince, it made her knees weak. "Your first loyalty is to your *trin-caar.*"

"That's it. I didn't mean to frighten you. I'm so sorry. That was completely uncalled for." He ran a hand over his short hair.

"You can make it up to me by letting me help." She lifted an eyebrow, forcing her gaze to stay on those burning violet eyes instead of drifting downward again. "That's all I really want—to get to the bottom of this."

"You're an uncommon woman, aren't you?"

Xaviara was taken aback. "What do you mean?"

"I thought at first you might only be interested in me because I'm posing as the prince. I've watched women fawn all over Camlan his entire life. Most of them don't care about him as a person. I finally got him to understand that years ago." The last part was muttered. "But you've known all along I'm not the prince. You're interested in *me.*"

Xaviara decided to be bold. "You intrigue me."

"Because I'm an alien?"

"Because you're well-traveled. A fighter. Sexy." Just the kind of man she was looking for, the complete opposite of Boring Tom.

His eyes widened. "You'll have to excuse me. Kadyyza women are forthright, but a different kind of forthright."

She'd seen the videos of purple- and blue-skinned women throwing themselves at Camlan. They were a people of action rather than words. His amazement was rather endearing. "This is new for me. I'm not usually forthright."

"I like it."

Xaviara shuddered.

"We probably shouldn't..." His eyes roamed over her body. "The treaty... And I can't relax until I know Camlan is safe."

Their eyes locked, and an electric shock of desire snapped through her. *Forthright, am I?* Deciding to seize the moment, Xaviara stepped forward and kissed him.

The warmth of him was delicious. She closed her eyes and leaned in, flicking a tongue across his bottom lip and moaning almost involuntarily. She was already slick from his heat against her, and she clenched at the sheer deliciousness of him.

He tasted like an exotic fruit from his solar system that she'd had once in preparation for this assignment. The outside was covered in spines she'd carefully pulled apart, but the inside was juicy and sweet. He met her fervor with passion of his own, pressing against her again. She reveled in the feel of him against her belly before pulling away.

His eyes were closed, his lips parted, and she leaned back against the wall to stop anything more from happening.

"You're right," she said.

His eyes fluttered open.

"We probably shouldn't." Heat crept from her hairline, over her cheeks, down her neck and past her breasts.

His hands clenched at his sides, as though he was willing himself not to grab her and push her against the wall again.

Before she gave in to the desire burning in his expression, Xaviara brushed past him toward the door. She hit the open button and waited as he blinked, swallowed, and stood up straight. The erection was now straining in his pants. If they were going to get out of this without breaking any more rules, they needed to go somewhere public.

"I'll give you a moment," she said. "I'll see what I can find out from the bridge, and then we can meet in the ship's library, start an investigation."

Nicholen looked like he was going to say something, but then just nodded.

"See you there in fifteen."

She gave him a wink—*so saucy, Xaviara,* completely unlike her—and swaggered out the door.

Chapter 7

Nicholen took the full fifteen minutes to get himself under control. The one perk of being thought the *trincaar* was that he had his own personal bathroom in which to splash over his face the most extremely cold water the tap could produce. He was probably using the entire trip's allotment, but he needed it.

Forebears, but Xaviara was an amazing woman. She was smart, sexy, and bolder than he'd expected her to be. She'd mostly faded into the background before, the picture-perfect junior delegate. The only things outstanding about her were her impeccable manners and obvious, intriguing knowledge of his culture. She was definitely destined for great things, and he was astounded that she'd taken an interest in him.

And her arousal was evident in the flowery bloom that his psy-sense manifested. It intoxicated him, lingering in his room even after she left. What he wouldn't give to have been able to slide those pants off her curves and lick her until she cried his name.

This wasn't helping his problem.

He knew full well that humans were off-limits until the treaty had been signed. In fact, he shouldn't be enlisting her help in finding the saboteur, but it had made sense when she'd asked: she knew the humans on board, and he wasn't sure which of the kadyyza he could trust. Who else on her team could he go to? Ah, but she had him in knots already.

He turned on the water higher and swallowed a gulp before splashing himself in the face again.

Finally, after too much cold water and too many thoughts of the last time he and Camlan practice fought—the most unsexy thing he could think of on short notice—he was ready to appear in public again. He adjusted his pants. From the way Xaviara had been eyeballing him, he was certain she'd seen exactly what she'd done to him.

Damn it, that's not helping.

Before his thoughts could go racing that way again, he pushed the door open button and strode into the hall.

The library was on the other side of the ship. It took most of his willpower not to stop by the bridge, but he knew if he ended up there, he'd jeopardize Camlan's secret. Despite the situation, he'd promised his prince to keep up the charade, and without an order to the contrary, he had no right to disclose it.

The library was a room lined with wallscreens and projected keyboards, used for more intense research purposes than links or the personal consoles in each room allowed. Just like the links, each connected up to the quanten network in the heart of the ship, allowing access to the wider net. Xaviara was sitting in front of one, typing away at a tablet, when he entered.

She said, "Everything seems to be under control on the planet, although we haven't been able to get through the planet's magnetic field to talk to them."

"Oh?" Nicholen's heart raced. He *hated* being out of control, and this situation was the epitome of that. He slid into a chair, and then for good measure, he reached over and tapped the door close button. It wasn't strictly polite to shut the door to a public space, but as *trincaar*—he smiled wryly—he could get away with it.

Plus he liked being trapped in a closed room with this woman, even if his every logical thought screamed that he should be running away.

Xaviara said, "They're still inside the ship. Gloria is attempting to establish real-time communication. She's keeping all channels open and monitoring their vitals when they get a break in the field. Everything seems to be going smoothly. She's doing all the right things."

Nicholen smacked a hand on the desk. "I wish I could *do* something."

Xaviara finally looked up. Her brown eyes pierced him. "We *are* doing something. This is the most important thing for your *trincaar*. If you want to get him out safe, you have to make sure you stop whatever the saboteur is planning."

"I know." It didn't make the raging frustration abate, though. "Where do you want to start?"

Xaviara swiped upward to push the image from her tablet to the wallscreen. "I used my security clearance to check whether the computer's automated security recorded anything unusual. I'm not able to get into everything, but I did find this. The audvid footage of the entire ship went dark moments before the ship fell out of mu-space."

Four scenes showed in each quadrant of the wallscreen: the bridge, the engine room, a hallway, and the mess hall. Then they went black.

"This continues for several minutes, and then it all comes back up. I've cycled through every camera in every location, and it's all the same."

"The saboteur didn't want to show his or her hand by blanking out only a few of the feeds." Clever. And it made their job even more difficult, of course. Through the haze of attraction for Xaviara, a thought was nagging him. He put a hand on hers, ignoring the spark that traveled up his arm to take root at the base of his neck. "How do I know you've not been sent to distract me?"

Xaviara's brown eyes met his. They dropped to his lips and jumped back up again. He kept himself tightly reined, not allowing wandering thoughts. She could merely be playing him for an advantage.

She said, "You don't."

The admission unwound something in him. He pulled his hand away. "How did you know I wasn't the real *trin-caar*?"

"I... don't know." Her hands fluttered over the tablet and came to rest in her lap. "As soon as you walked in the room, I felt ill. Everything went watery. I thought I was having a bout of food poisoning. When the world righted itself, I saw you wearing the *trincaar*'s cape, but I remembered your dossier. You're the captain. I knew it for sure."

She seemed so confused and vulnerable. Nicholen had interrogated hundreds of people over the years, and he knew a liar when he met one. He might not always know what the lie was, but he could tell when a person was hiding something.

Xaviara was not.

"I don't know what else to tell you." She shrugged. "If you want me out of here, I'll go. You can even have my tablet with my security access to the Sol Alliance Coalition database. I've already broken one of the rules," her eyes flicked to his lips again, "so I might as well break more of them."

Fuck, he didn't want to be in this position, but he had to decide. He could trust her, work with her, breathe in her delicious scent while they tried to figure out the true saboteur—or he could send her out of the room right now and go it alone.

He did not want to go it alone.

Am I letting my cock make the decisions for me? Except he wasn't—he knew very well they couldn't have a relationship. As if to underscore it to himself, he said aloud, "We can't have a relationship."

"No, we can't," she answered. "I could get fired."

He would likely fare better—an official reprimand from Camlan, delivered in a joking manner—but he didn't want to jeopardize *her* job. "No more kissing."

"No more kissing."

"Or anything else."

"Or anything," she blushed, "else."

How long is that *going to last?*

"I believe you're not the saboteur," he said, hoping he wouldn't regret it later. He would keep his bullshit detector on high alert, and anything out of the ordinary, he'd be sure to take action on. "Do you have any inkling as to who it might be?"

The pink was fading from Xaviara's cheeks. "I started researching the humans on board since I have more information on them than the kadyyza. I've come up with one strong suspect so far, but you're not going to like it."

"Why? Who is it?" This was not calming him.

She looked up, her long hair spilling down the back of the chair. "It's Gloria."

"The Senior Ambassador who's worked for the Sol Alliance Coalition as a diplomat for twenty-five years?" Yeah, he'd done his background checks. "The one who you just assured me is doing everything she can to get Camlan off the planet?"

"Yes. As much as I really don't like the woman, I don't want it to be her either. That's why I said she seems to be doing everything she should. If it *is* her, she's at least going through the motions. But what I found seems so glaring."

"And what is that?"

"The rest of the team is way too junior to pull off a sabotage of this magnitude."

"She did come onto the bridge *after* the disaster, but she had no reason to be there before it happened," he mused. "But what's her motive?"

"I don't know yet. I just began investigating her when you walked in. I started by running through the other eleven humans on board since I have access to their internal profiles. None of the others seem capable of this. That fact alone makes Gloria a suspect because she's the only one with clearance level Lambda. The next closest clearance level is Theta."

"Three below hers."

"You know your human security clearances."

"It's my job to know," Nicholen said.

"Fair enough." Xaviara tapped her fingers on the side of the tablet. "And that's the thing. If I didn't know any better, I'd say she hand-picked this team to be as junior as possible without arousing suspicion in her higher-ups. Even the fact that she put Manda in charge is odd. Don't get me wrong, I admire her—she's a good boss, maybe even something of a friend—but this is not the kind of delegation you have a Junior Ambassador leading."

"She was so determined to get me off the bridge." He didn't like this. He didn't like it at all. "I need to take over the rescue effort."

"Not yet," said Xaviara.

"What do you mean?" He wasn't used to anyone disagreeing with him—except, perhaps, the *trincaarit*.

"If it *is* her, you don't want to tip her off. We need more information. I'll see if I can find a motive first." She tapped to swap from her notes to another program. "I've started a search for any pieces of information that seem out of the ordinary. The AI should be able to find something based on my parameters."

"Like... ?" Nicholen was good at surveillance, in-person interviews, and detecting mechanical failures—which meant he was still kicking himself over missing whatever caused the lead ship to crash. Xaviara's savvy with computers impressed him.

"Out-of-system trips that weren't tied to diplomatic missions. Monetary transactions that were out of the ordinary. Even public displays of support on her social media channels for any dubious organizations."

"Anything so far?"

"No. I mean, I just started it. It'll take about an hour to complete."

He didn't want to wait. "I don't know about this." He was itching to leap up, storm onto the bridge, and order the older woman into the brig.

"Isn't it possible that the saboteur could be a kadyyza? They're the ones who know the prince is actually on the planet."

Nicholen's muscles were taut with frustration, but her logic stopped him from leaping out of the chair. "I suppose you're right." What if it *was* one of his own people? Camlan would have chided him for his lack of loyalty toward his own species, but Nicholen had been doing this job long enough to know that Imdali produced just as many security threats as any other place.

"It seems dangerous for them to know about that swap."

"Maybe. I do a thorough background check on all new team members, though. There's only one I don't trust." *And fuck, do I not trust her.* He took the tablet from her and punched into the Imdali internal database. "...Verrytto Lianndra. Camlan and I have argued more times than I can count about her. He insists she's a skilled diplomat and grateful for her job. We always end with the same conclusion: until I can find a shred of evidence she's doing anything wrong, he's not going to kick her off the team."

"Why? Who is she?"

He wasn't sure if he was smiling or grimacing. "His ex-girlfriend. They dated for years back when they were in university together. And there's no love lost between them, especially with how he's been playing up his playboy image lately."

Chapter 8

"That's pretty strong motive," said Xaviara. "An ex-girlfriend?" It seemed so reckless, but it fit with the image of the *trincaar* she'd picked up from her research.

"That's why I keep trying to convince Camlan to drop her." He shook his head. "Kid won't ever learn."

Xaviara couldn't stop the giggle that escaped her. "Kid? You two are the same age."

His eyebrow raised. "You certainly know a lot about us."

"It's my job."

"Fair point, but you don't have to know everything. Aides are pretty low on the totem pole."

Her stomach dropped. Is that what he thought of her? "I won't always be." The words came out harsher than she'd meant, but his assertion chafed. Everyone had to start somewhere, and she was still young—barely into her twenties.

"I didn't mean anything by that."

"Fine. Whatever. Anyone else I should know about? Unless you think I'm too far beneath your notice to help out anymore." She'd been a fool to kiss him like that back in his room, especially given all she was risking. After all, he might not be a prince, but he was head of a prince's security detail. Far above her station. She should just stick with local guards, if she could find one who wasn't attempting to thwart an important human alliance.

"No, that's not what I—" His eyebrows furrowed.

She shrugged and looked down at the tablet where Lianndra's internal dossier was still displayed. Nicholen went still and unmoving, but she wasn't going to speak first. If he wanted her to understand who was senior, well, message received loud and clear. She was excellent at following orders. If that's what it took to get Manda off the planet, she could do that.

He finally spoke. "Look, I don't have much experience dating. This job has been my focus for years. I'm terrible talking with kadyyza women, let alone someone of another species."

Wait, I thought he said we couldn't—

He reached out a hand and placed it on hers again. Electricity crackled through her, coming to rest as an ache between her legs. "I really didn't mean anything by it," he said. "I'm sorry. I don't see you as lesser."

She turned her hand over, feeling his warmth against her. Tracing a finger along his wrist, she bit her lip. If she looked at him, she might do something they'd both just agreed couldn't happen. She willed herself still, hoping he would pull his hand away and longing for him not to.

When he kissed her, she was so surprised, she kept her eyes open. His eyelashes fluttered, catching the light, and his tongue dipped into her mouth, dancing quickly across the tip of hers.

As her eyes closed, his hand brushed over her hair, combing down and through the long locks. She returned the kiss, but he refused to allow her control, keeping himself leaning forward and letting her melt. Desire thrilled through her and ended in a tiny shudder when he pulled away.

"If you think kissing me is going to make up for the insult..." she started.

"Of course not." His grin was disarming, and any fake indignation she was trying to muster evaporated. "I'm sure I'll spend quite a long time trying to make it up to you."

"See that you do." Her chest squeezed. He clearly knew this was forbidden, but he was moving forward with it anyway. What would Manda say? Did Xaviara even care? She cleared her throat. "In the meantime, you were giving me a rundown of all our suspects."

"Jessan has been serving the royal family since Camlan's grandfather was *trincaarit*. I honestly can't see her betraying him any more than his own grandmother. Our pilot is new, but he's a member of the military with fairly high security clearance. Now, our chief engineer..." He held out his hand for the tablet and pulled up the man's profile. "I got an odd feeling from him when I was doing interviews for this delegation."

"And you let him in anyway?"

"He was highly sought after, so Camlan insisted, but his emotions seemed erratic. He was up and down and all over the place. I didn't like it."

How interesting. She couldn't help but pry. "It's rumored that kadyyza can read minds. Or is that only the royal family?"

He gave her a long look. "Nobody can read minds. We sense emotion."

Her breath caught. "And what kind of emotion do you sense in me?"

"Breniel Brashhre." His smile seemed almost mischievous.

"What?"

"That's his name. Breniel Brashhre."

Was he regretting the kiss? But no—the look in his eyes was lustful, not regretful. *Fine, two can play the coy game.* She said, "Anyone else you can think of?"

"Not right now. Lianndra has the best motive—revenge—and Breniel has the best opportunity, being the chief engineer. I might be an excellent security chief, but he was top of his class. He'd be able to hide something from me if he really wanted to."

Xaviara leapt to her feet, uncoiling some of the pent-up energy he'd awakened in her. "What are we waiting for? Let's go talk to them."

* * *

Nicholen loved the way Xaviara took charge of a situation. She was a natural born leader, and the Sol Alliance Coalition was lucky to have her. Someday—probably sooner than anyone thought—she'd be running a delegation like this of her own. However, he needed to be careful if he ever decided to let thoughts like that sneak out of his mouth. He'd already seen her fiery temper flare, and he wasn't about to piss off this gorgeous woman, who was becoming more attractive to him with every passing moment.

But they needed to be cautious. "Wait," he said.

Her hand was poised over the button to open the door.

"You and I— We're not supposed to— If we—" *Out with it, man.* "I think you should stay back and watch the security audvid." He pointed to her tablet. "We can't be seen together."

She pressed her lips into a tight line. "I suppose you're right." Her look said she didn't like it. "I'll go to my room and pull up the engine room feed."

She led the way down the hall, hips swaying in a sexy rhythm that made him wonder if she had a particularly interesting song in her head. Her feelings wafted as a cloud of fruity-smelling goodness—she was pleased with herself, though for what, he could only guess. Psychic indeed. That would take the guesswork out of his job, and maybe Camlan wouldn't be in this mess.

When she veered off down the hallway, he almost didn't mind since he got to watch her leave. With a tightening in his groin, he turned down the corridor and hurried toward the engine room.

Outside the door, the thrumming was quiet. Inside, though, it was loud enough that he had to shout.

"Breniel?" he called past the rounded, sleek engine in the middle.

A tall, blocky kadyyza popped his head from around the corner. "Ah! Captain!"

"Hey! Anyone could be listening," Nicholen reminded him. He might not like this duty, but it was his to carry out. Breniel was the only kadyyza senior member of the crew of the anchor ship; two human engineers were stationed in the engine room with him.

"Sorry." Breniel dipped his head. "Forgot. *Trincaar.* What can I do for you?"

"Were you able to review the ship's diagnostics from before we lost contact with them? I'm curious what caused it to spin off course like that."

Nicholen had been unsure about Breniel, even though his background check was spotless. During the interview, his emotions were difficult to understand, and that continued now. He smelled first of engine grease, then a warm summer's morning, then a quick whiff of rancid meat. Each one alone would have had its own interpretation, but cycling through them so quickly made it difficult to tell what he was feeling.

After too long of a pause, Breniel spoke. "I did review the diagnostics. I do know what caused it to spin off course like that."

"And?" Every conversation with him went like this. It was as though he resented Nicholen's interest in his work.

But it was Nicholen's job as security chief to know the ins and outs of every part of the ship.

Breniel pressed a button on the console nearest his head. Up came a diagram of the mu-engine on the lead ship. "You see here? A subatomic leak occurred in the superconducting pump. The neutron core became polarized, and the magnetic storm made the navigation unstable. When we came within the mu-radius of planet UTP-8907, its strong magnetic field further added to the problem."

"And how did the leak happen?"

"I don't know."

"Wear and tear?" asked Nicholen.

"Most likely no."

The words hung in the air between them. Breniel's scent was now fully engine grease—a pleasant smell that indicated he was happy with his assessment.

"Thank you for your time, Chief Engineer." Nicholen strode to the door, wondering what Xaviara would make of that conversation.

He was at her door in moments. It opened to reveal her at her console. He looked to the left, glanced to the right, and stepped inside.

"Quite the ruse in there," she said as the door slid shut.

"I'm not sure it was a ruse."

"What better way to throw you off track than to admit exactly how he'd sabotaged the ship?"

"I didn't sense he was trying to hide anything." He wasn't sure *what* he'd sensed. "He's always difficult to read."

"If he knew you would know if he was lying, he'd use that to cover it up."

"True enough. But my psy-sense doesn't work like that."

She looked back at wallscreen, which displayed Breniel at work on the engine. "I suppose that's all right. You have two more suspects to talk to. Come on, I want to see this ex-girlfriend of Camlan's."

Oh, boy. Now that would be an interesting conversation.

Chapter 9

Watching Nicholen interact with Breniel was fascinating to Xaviara. She loved seeing him at work—he was clearly in his element, interrogating a suspect. Breniel's stance and quick answers revealed that he respected the Captain of the Guard, but he seemed to be uncomfortable. Plus his eyes kept returning to the bank of consoles behind Nicholen. Was he hiding something? Waiting for a message? Eager to get back to work?

She decided not to push it, preferring to see Nicholen with their other two suspects before they finished comparing notes.

Xaviara pulled up the cramped mess hall on the wallscreen. Four of the five tables were full, and Xaviara's fellow aides Rosa, Piotr, and Kristoph huddled along the back wall. Rosa was laughing, Kristoph was telling an animated story, and Piotr was smirking while tracing his finger over his wrist tattoo, the infinity symbol surrounded by a circle. She almost felt a strain of jealousy—Piotr also seemed to be attempting to befriend the other two, at her expense—but then decided she'd rather be working with Nicholen any day.

Nicholen glanced up at the camera, and she warmed at the thought of having a secret they shared. He inclined his head toward a table, indicating where Lianndra sat with Jessan and two kadyyza aides Xaviara had had brief interactions with. Their plates were mostly empty, and all four lounged with the posture of someone who'd finished a satisfying meal.

Xaviara adjusted the audio to pick up the conversation in that corner.

Nicholen squared his shoulders and marched toward the table. His bearing changed. With Breniel and even Gloria earlier, his back had been straight, but now he seemed to be bracing for something.

Lianndra was laughing an open-mouthed laugh when he stopped at the head of their table. "That is *great*," she was saying to Jessan. "I can't believe he fell for that."

"Who fell for what?" Nicholen's first words were much less self-assured than Xaviara had heard before.

"Don't worry about it, Nich." Lianndra didn't look up at him. "Nothing to do with you."

He seemed to flounder, then drew himself tall again. "I'd like a word."

"About what?"

"The crash."

"We're in the middle of dinner," she said, still grinning.

Jessan and the aides had fallen silent, their faces not full of the mirth Lianndra's held.

"May I?" said Nicholen to the closest aide. "You're done, anyway."

"Look, *trincaar*," the sarcasm behind the word was overt, "it's rude to interrupt a meal."

Nicholen's face was darkening, but before he could answer, Jessan pushed herself standing. "Come along. Let's leave these two to talk." She addressed Lianndra. "Don't be rude. He's your *trincaar*." That word was loaded with overtones, not the least of which was an admonishment that she needed to respect Nicholen's true station.

Xaviara's eyes darted between the older and younger women. Jessan's mouth was drawn into a thin line, and Lianndra's lip stuck out in almost a pout. She finally waved a hand. "Go. We were done anyway."

Without a word, the aides scurried after Jessan, who gracefully swept from the room.

What a piece of work. Xaviara didn't have to be a Senior anything of anything to detect *that*.

Nicholen slid into the seat across from Lianndra.

"I thought the humans were working on the rescue." Lianndra wasn't looking at her newest companion.

"Yes, but it doesn't hurt to approach the problem from several angles."

"True," her mouth lifted in a sneer, "and I'd rather have a kadyyza on it than trust the problem to outsiders."

Xaviara was starting to see why Nicholen didn't like her—brusque, rude, and a barely contained xenophobe to boot. What did Camlan see in this woman to allow her on diplomatic missions?

"I was just in the engine room going over the results from the crash with Breniel." Nicholen voice was low, almost a growl. "I found something interesting."

"Did you?" The words were tossed out casually, but Xaviara detected interest in her tone.

"We believe the ship was sabotaged. What do you know about that?"

"Me?" She barked her loud laugh again. "Nothing."

"Ah. Well. Where were you this afternoon between fourteen and fifteen hundred hours?"

Even Lianndra's eye roll was exaggerated. "Is this how it's going to be? Honestly, Nicholen, I don't know why you're wasting your time on me when you could be hunting down the real culprit."

"You know why," he said quietly.

"Just because I cheated on the guy doesn't mean I want to strand him on a wild planet."

"Twice." Nicholen punctuated the word with his thumb and pointer. "You cheated on him twice."

"And if I wanted to kill him, I could have done so a thousand times over. I have no reason to go out of my way to create such an elaborate scenario."

Nicholen's face was turning more stormy than it had before. "And I'm supposed to believe that someone who so casually speaks of killing our... captain... is innocent of sabotaging this entire mission?"

"You always were so over-dramatic. Camlan's well over what happened. Why can't you get over it, too?"

Nicholen slammed a hand down on the table. Xaviara jumped, but Lianndra's smirk merely widened. "Watch yourself!"

Xaviara was starting to wonder if she would need to hurry down there and break up a fist fight when Nicholen leapt from his seat.

"That's it. I'm going," he said. "I will find out what you did, Lianndra. I will find it out, and I will finally have what I need to prove to Camlan that you're a lying *jixxis*, like you were all those years ago."

"Little ol' me knows nothing about engineering. Besides, this is a good gig. Why would I want to ruin something that's working for me?"

Nicholen clenched a fist. "I'll figure out who did it. And I'll make them pay."

"See that you do. Despite all that, I *am* rather fond of Camlan. I was just never a one-man girl." She was studying her fingernails now.

With a huff, Nicholen marched from the mess hall.

Chapter 10

Xaviara waited for Nicholen to appear at her door, but he didn't. She waited... and waited... And finally, she pushed back from the desk and hurried toward the kadyyza section. A lone aide sauntered past her, and she pretended to keep going past the red *trincaar*'s door. When she was alone, she scurried back and pressed the doorbell.

"Come in." The door slid open to reveal Nicholen hunched over the desk, multiple screens open on the console open in front of him. *Is he doing paperwork?* He was staring at it like it contained all the secrets of the universe, but he didn't flip a page or type anything. The prince's jacket and cape were tossed on the bed, and he wore only a shirt made of light, thin fabric that clung tightly to his chest muscles.

"Sometimes," he said, "the worst part about the humans thinking I'm *trincaar* is them thinking I dated that... that..."

Before someone could wander past and see her inside the room, Xaviara pushed the door close button. She sat on the bed, pushing aside the clothes, a thrill coursing through her at being in proximity to where he would sleep tonight. "You and Camlan are close."

Nicholen ran a hand over his hair. Xaviara's fingers curled into her leg. In such close quarters, the sexual energy was back. She wanted to reach over and run her fingers over it herself, but instead, she waited for him to respond.

"Yes, we're close," he said. "We grew up together. My father is head of the *trincaarit*'s security force—retiring soon but still going strong. I admired him so much growing up. Still do, of course. So when I came of age, I went into the military to train. When my tour of duty was finished, I became part of Camlan's security force and now I'm the Captain of his Guard. It's an honor to serve this way, especially for a man who's been through so much."

"Being *trincaar* isn't easy, I suppose. Especially after losing your older brother and being thrust into the position." Xaviara knew all about Willex's drowning death.

"You know our backgrounds well." Nicholen swiveled toward her. "It's my duty to protect him, and I couldn't. Not from that. Not from this crash. And not from Lianndra."

Xaviara's heart broke a little for the prince who was stranded on a planet, but it broke more for a man who seemed to be carrying the weight of his solar system on his shoulders.

"It all happened when I was away." Nicholen closed down the program he was working on. "She cheated on him soon after I left. They broke up, of course. She told him she was sorry, they got back together... Then it happened again. I *told* him not to get back together with her! I told him but he didn't listen. And I was halfway across the system. I couldn't do anything."

"You wouldn't have been able to do anything if you were there." Xaviara spoke quietly, unsure how her words were going to be taken, but wanting to do something to help. Beneath the gruff exterior and fiery temper, Nicholen had a heart of gold. If only she could soothe away his stress... But they'd agreed not to pursue a relationship. Hadn't they? The second kiss had muddled things, especially since she found herself wanting things she shouldn't.

"Maybe I could have stopped him from getting hurt. I tell myself that this is partly my fault."

"The sabotage?"

"No, no..." He sighed. "I don't think she did it."

Xaviara sat back. "Really?"

"She's definitely a manipulator, but she has a coveted job. Why would she risk it? What would she gain? She might not be with Camlan any more, but *she* cheated on *him*. And then he gave her a great job. Most qualified, pah. What's she got to be bitter about?"

"So what do you blame yourself for?" she asked.

"Everything. He *says* he forgave her, but after his brother's death, he was embracing being the oldest, learning how to be *trincaarit*. Then *that* happened once, and then again. The way he treats women now—the goofing around for the neural net vids, the flirting—it's not Camlan. I should have stopped it. I'm his oldest friend, his protector. He should never have taken her back."

"Nicholen, this is not your fault. You couldn't have stopped it. It was his decision. If you'd been there in person, it might have caused a rift in your relationship. People have to make their own decisions concerning love."

His face was anguished, and Xaviara soon found herself on her knees, taking his hand in hers.

He said, "I'm his Captain of the Guard. If I couldn't stop it, who could have?"

"It wasn't your job to stop it."

Xaviara wasn't sure he'd told her everything. "What is this really about?"

His gaze flickered downward. She didn't think he would answer, but then he said, quietly, "I'm responsible for the future *trincaarit*. What if the same thing happens to Camlan that happened to Willex?"

"It won't."

"But what if it does?"

"It won't," said Xaviara, "because you'll be there."

The relief on his face was like a ray of sunlight breaking through a cloud. "You really think... ?"

"I do. Look how hard you're working to find the saboteur. You'd do anything to protect him."

"I would."

"And so you will."

His hand was warm and large, enveloping hers even as she tried to comfort him. He squeezed her fingers gently, shooting waves of desire through her core. She looked up at him, eyes wide, drinking in his handsome face and dark hair. She'd never have thought she would fall for a man of another species, but he was so strong and earnest, hard and soft in equal measures, though perhaps he would never want to admit it.

The door was closed. No one knew they were in here. He'd kissed her even after telling her they shouldn't. He wanted more.

And so did she.

Excitement shivered down her spine at the idea of how forbidden this was. She sat up, grabbed his shirt, and pulled him toward her. He complied with the unspoken command, and she lifted her lips to his and softly brushed them together. Tingles shot through her, warming her to her toes.

Before she could talk herself out of it, she stood and slid into his lap, straddling him.

His tongue found hers, and she placed her hands on either side of his chest and ran them up his neck to the sides of his face. "But," he mumbled, "what if—"

"Shhhh," she whispered back and kept kissing him. She wanted to do something to comfort him. She wanted to make him feel better. She couldn't stand to see him suffer.

He smiled against her mouth and went back to kissing her. Beneath her fingers, the tension fell away from his shoulders, and he leaned back in the chair.

"Should we... ?" he started.

"Do you want to?"

Violet eyes held lust for her, and his bulge answered for him.

"I can leave right now," she said.

"I don't want you to."

"Neither do I."

Their mouths met. His tongue battled hers. But she'd already decided: *No, saucy boy, this is for you.* Xaviara was emboldened. She was falling for this man, despite how much trouble it might cause her, and he was hurting. She needed to do something. No matter how this turned out—if they ended up together or had a one-time fling—she wanted him to know that he was unique and special in this world of cheaters and saboteurs.

Her hands slid down his torso.

* * *

Nicholen's blood roared as Xaviara kissed him. He was used to being in charge—but he loved that she was taking the lead. Her hands slid slowly down his chest, heating him up from the inside. His member raged to attention, straining against where she straddled his hips. She shifted, allowing him to spring up, and then pressed herself against him, trapping him with delicious heat.

He wanted her more than he'd ever wanted another woman, rules be damned. Perhaps the forbidden nature of this tryst made him want it all the more. He'd given his life to this career for so many years, it was time he took something back.

Her hands finished their journey. She rocked her hips back enough to catch him and encircle his length with deft, strong fingers. She paused only to wrangle him free of the light fabric pants. With his manhood exposed to the cool air, she continued the up and down strokes. He tried reaching for her pants, but she batted his hands away.

Her intention was clear: she wanted to pleasure him. "Umm," he said.

"Shhh," she replied. Her scent was fruity and floral, intoxicating to his psy-sense. She was aroused and pleased, and he wanted to devour her.

No, he couldn't simply let her... But she was *amazing* at that...

She stood and the heat of her vanished. With one hand on his shaft and one hands on his pants, she tugged at the fabric. "Lift your hips."

Still fighting for the right objection, he obliged. Soon they were pooled around his ankles.

In a flash, she was on her knees, kissing his torso without removing a hand from where she gripped him. Every stroke sent waves of pleasure from his belly to his balls.

"I can't let you," he said. "Let me. Please." Forebears, he didn't want her to stop, but he wasn't used to taking without giving back.

"Don't be silly," Xaviara said between kisses. "I already know you're a gentleman. My turn will come. Won't it?" Her mouth was moving closer to his cock, and her hand never stopped moving on his length.

"But what does it mean?" he managed to gasp out.

"It means I want to do this for you. Lean back."

And with that last admonishment, her warm, soft lips covered his head, her hand squeezed down his shaft, and her other hand rolled his balls back and forth between her fingers.

He'd run out of protestations. Xaviara was a force of nature. She got what she wanted, and what she wanted, apparently, was to—

"Ohhhh," he growled. Her tongue was *amazing*. Just like the rest of her.

The rules only covered an active delegation. Once the treaty was signed, they could pursue a relationship. And he badly wanted to see more of this woman. She was strong, smart, sexy, bold, and—

She sucked in his length, and all thoughts of anything but Xaviara's mouth fled from his mind. He was lost in her, all focus on his rigid cock. It had been so long since he'd been pleasured in this way, he'd almost forgotten how delicious it was. Her mouth was so hot... Her grip was so tight...

Xaviara grabbed his hand and put it on the back of her head, sending waves of pleasure searing through him. She bobbed up and down, faster now, tongue swirling in complex patterns that sent him higher and higher. He wanted to draw this out—the feel of her mouth on him, the look she was giving him from between his knees.

He couldn't hold on. He was rising, testicles contracting. "I'm going to..."

She squeezed and sucked hard, and he came into her mouth, seed bursting from his manhood. His hand groped through her hair as the rest of his body went rigid. She was swallowing, sucking, swallowing, as he pulsed and groaned and threw his head back.

And then he was relaxing—looking down at that saucy glint in her deep brown eyes. She let him drop from her mouth and said, "I certainly hope that made you feel better."

Coming back from the haze, he let out a strangled laugh. "Oh, it did. It definitely did."

But it wasn't only the blowjob. It was her belief in his capability. Her actions spoke as loud as her words: they would find the saboteur together and stop whoever it was. She had absolutely no doubt in him.

Chapter 11

Xaviara laid on the bed, arms wrapped around Nicholen. A familiar ache between her legs tantalized her. He'd tried to repay her, but she wanted to wait, preferring instead to snuggle up next to him as he laid in a blissful half-stupor from what *she* had done.

Whatever happened with the investigation, she'd make sure he paid her back. Besides, he was still sighing periodically and saying, "That was amazing. You didn't have to do that." She'd long since stopped trying to dissuade him from making that assertion. It was true. She *didn't* have to. And that knowledge made her feel sexy, strong, and close to him as they cuddled together.

Despite how perfect she felt, her thoughts returned to the problem at hand. Gloria had all but ordered Nicholen from the bridge to allow the human team to deal with the stranded lead ship, and she wouldn't take too kindly to being questioned by the *trincaar* she saw as superfluous. But he needed to talk to her—needed to deploy his interrogation skills to pull out any additional information she might have.

Xaviara couldn't think of a pleasant way to break through Nicholen's blissful reverie. She glanced up at his face. His eyes were hooded, a lazy smile making him even more handsome than she remembered. Shivering, she opened her mouth.

Her tablet beeped three long beeps.

Xaviara pushed herself from Nicholen's chest. The lazy look was gone, although the smile still flitted at the corners of his mouth. "What's that?" he asked.

She swung herself over the edge of the bed. "The scan is done. And it found something of interest on Gloria."

He sat bolt upright, chest muscles contracting underneath the thin fabric, his shirt pushed halfway up his belly. Despite what had just gone on, Xaviara couldn't help but trace the light line of hair down his chest and past his naval. He caught her look and grinned almost shyly. *It's a little late for that.* She loved how adorable he was, rubbing his hand over the back of his neck and looking sheepish.

She tore her eyes away reluctantly. "Let me see what it says."

Opening the tablet, she pulled up the program. She'd already queued up the next search string, so she started it right away. It was an algorithm that would detect any similar clues amongst the other humans. The search was broader and would take more time, which is why she had started the Gloria search first. The hourglass came up, signaling the search was running, so she switched over to the results.

Nicholen was looking at her anxiously, though he lounged backward onto his pillow. Xaviara bit her lip and focused on the tablet, willing herself not to let her mind go wandering off into delectable memories. "It says here that she has some investments we need to look at."

"Investments? What are they?"

Xaviara opened the results window for more details. "Oh. Oh! Oh..."

"I can't wait to make you make those noises later, little *viaar*," Nicholen's voice was low and sultry, "but you can't keep a guy in suspense like that."

She could feel a blush creeping over her face. *Even after what we just did?* "Gloria has stock in PDJ Holdings, Inc."

"PDJ Holdings? Unfortunately, I'm only the pretend *trincaar*. Camlan might know what that is, but I can't keep all those diplomatic details in my head."

"It's the rival corporation to the one who won the contract to mine the space anomaly for the humans after this contract is signed." Xaviara gasped. "And it's a *lot* of stock. Gloria, you really should have diversified."

Nicholen pushed himself upright. "So once this treaty completes, the company's stock is going to lose money?"

"It already has, but yes, essentially. If she can halt this treaty, that would give PDJ time to make a deal with Ice, Limited, who won the contract, or maybe challenge their bid altogether. I mean, they've already challenged and lost, but..." She flipped through the detailed results.

"Look, it says here that she's been gathering these stocks since she was young. It looks like the first one was bought twenty-eight years ago."

"There must be a reason for that."

She tabbed back to the search list. "An uncle who's a Senior Vice President at PDJ."

"That's the perfect motive. And she has the means, with all the security clearances." Nicholen pulled the sheet up his torso. "She wouldn't necessarily need to do it herself. She could lend her clearance to one of her underlings and have them enact whatever the plan was."

"Yes..."

"Did she ever hint about your loyalties?" His voice turned stern—clearly he was back in security mode.

"No." Xaviara had little interaction with the woman. Most of it was through Manda. And she didn't want to talk about her embarrassing rivalry with Piotr. "I was hoping to get back into her good graces after what happened with Boring Tom."

Nicholen raised an eyebrow. "Boring Tom?"

She laughed. "Yeah, sorry, that's what I call him in my head. The guy I was on a date with, who got that suspicious mail."

Nicholen bristled. "Ah. Boring Tom."

"Jealous?" she teased.

"No... No!" His grin was sly. "Do you have a nickname for me?"

She cocked her head to the side. "How about Super-Sizzlin' Nicholen? It doesn't quite rhyme, but—"

He guffawed. "I love it. Come here." He held out a hand.

She stood and took it. He pulled her into him, and they tumbled onto the bed, laughing. His kiss was long, passionate, and full of promises that he wasn't going to forget the debt he owed. *Good. He'd better not.* She smiled into the kiss, and he rolled her over to give her neck a nuzzle.

"All right," she gasped, "what are we going to do with this information? We'd better do something before night falls below."

"We already did something." Nicholen pulled away from her neck, propping himself on his hands, and letting his hips drop to grind against hers. "Want to do something more?"

"Oh, stop." She was breathless. "I mean about your stranded prince."

That sobered him. "I doubt Camlan would be so reckless as to leave the ship overnight. At least not the first night. But you're right. We'd better get to the bridge."

He kissed her again, flicking his tongue across hers and lingering long enough that she could feel the stirring of his hard-on. Before she could change her mind—*after all, who wants to wait for dessert?*—he pushed himself up and off the bed.

She groaned. "All right. But you'd better not forget that you owe me one."

As he reached to the floor to pick up his shirt, his sexy smile shot liquid desire straight through her body.

* * *

Xaviara was something else. Nicholen didn't know what to think of her, although he could spend hours upon hours doing so. But they had a job to do. After checking that the hallway was clear, he let her scurry out the door in front of him, watching the sway of her hips and her little sidelong once-over.

As they made their way to the bridge, his head cleared. They had to do something about Gloria, although he didn't know what. She was going to be unhappy no matter what he said when they got to the bridge. He *did* have some authority here as *trincaar*, although it was a sticky situation.

Camlan had never anticipated that he wouldn't be around to back up Nicholen's decisions as the true *trincaar*, so everything Nicholen asserted now was unsupported. He doubted any of the kadyyza would challenge his decisions. It helped that he was Captain of the Guard, so they were used to listening to him—even irritating Lianndra begrudgingly paid him respect when she had to.

With that line of thought opened an entirely new wellspring of frustration, but he pushed it aside.

Lost in thought, he almost walked onto the bridge, but Xaviara held out a hand to stop him. "What are you going to do?"

His hand hovered over the door open button. "I'm not sure. I need to confront her, but..."

"... but this is perhaps a job for diplomacy."

"Diplomacy? Or brute strength?"

"What?" Xaviara's eyes widened.

"I could throw Gloria into the brig. Take over the rescue mission on my authority as *trincaar*." He activated his link. "Thoxxin, Kalliph, meet me at the bridge."

She tugged on his sleeve. "Are you sure she did it, then?"

"Reasonably sure. I don't think it's Lianndra, and I suspect Breniel less than her."

"So, no?"

"Let me get a status update, and then I'll decide. We know she has the means and motive, and it wouldn't have been hard to create the opportunity. Okay?"

Xaviara looked down the empty hallway, suddenly unsure. "What if she finds out I'm helping you?" His psysense picked up a chilly scent, like the air after a cold rainstorm.

Something bright flared in Nicholen's chest, a fierce protectiveness for this woman. If this were true, they were going into the den of a predator who had control over her life and livelihood. And in post-coital bliss, he'd just walked through the ship with her at his side. *Fuck, man, think!* "I won't stand for any repercussions against you, no matter what happens."

"I like you, Nicholen. A lot. Enough to risk whatever trouble I could get into," she whispered.

"If I turn out to be wrong, I'll be the one to take the blame. And I will use all of my resources as *trincaar*," he smiled wryly, "and after, as Captain of the Guard, to ensure that this doesn't come back on you."

"Thank you."

His guards would be here any minute, but despite that, he kissed her fiercely, stirring a longing that would never be sated. He pulled away. "Do you want to watch from your room?"

She shook her head. "I'll wait a couple seconds and then come in."

He nodded and punched the door open button.

* * *

Nicholen pulled himself to his full height, and Xaviara sighed inwardly at how commanding he was. That declaration meant he felt more for her than this sexual chemistry zinging between them. He wanted *her*.

On the bridge, Gloria was bent over a console, giving directions to the communication officer, Samantha. "Keep trying," she said. "We'll break through eventually."

"Any progress?" Nicholen's voice was gruff, but he walked in like he owned the ship. Briefly, Xaviara wondered if he would act this way when acting as Captain of the Guard, but then—remembering how awkward he seemed at first playing the *trincaar*—realized this was his true self shining through.

She couldn't wait to get him back into the bedroom and have a true matching of equals.

Gloria's face was neutral as he approached. "We have not yet been able to break through the planet's magnetic field and get a message to the ship below."

"And have they sent us anything?"

"We've been monitoring all channels, but nothing so far."

"That's disappointing." Nicholen strode to the console and brushed aside the communication officer. "Let me take a look."

Xaviara recognized the program he was booting up. It was a raw review of all the information the ship was taking in. During a space voyage, massive amounts of data were collected by starships—locations of systems, radio signals that usually ended up being neutron stars, and any other random information that was passing through.

That information was uploaded to a central body that sorted through it and used it to create more accurate space maps. One of her classes in university was how to parse through the information, but unfortunately, she'd not been great at differentiating the code-like strings of data at the time, and she'd forgotten most of it now.

Nicholen was scrolling through the information, pausing, and then scrolling again. It was impressive how quickly he was reading it, but then, the Captain of the Guard would have reason to monitor all communications going in and out of the ship, even mundane ones. To the computer, he said, "Override previous commands with security clearance for Valkkh Nicholen."

"Excuse me," said Gloria, "but we've been monitoring the commdump, and we haven't found anything."

A staticky voice broke out over the overhead speakers. "Anchor ship... is lead ship... crash-landed... following coordinates... Repeat."

Nicholen pinned Gloria with his gaze. "Haven't found anything? It's right here." To Samantha, he said, "Clean up that transmission and compile a response."

Gloria's mouth flopped open. "Now wait a minute. *I* am in charge of this mission."

"Gloria Falchuk of the Sol Alliance Coalition, I am invoking my right as Imdali System *trincaar* to remove you from your position as interim Lead. You are being accused of treasonous acts against peaceful diplomatic delegation KH-159, and I am ordering your confinement to the brig."

The two kadyyza officers Nicholen had summoned appeared at the doorway. Gloria's head snapped to look at them. "What? That's ridiculous! I—"

"I don't want to hear more about it. Lock her up. I'm taking over this rescue operation."

Nicholen flicked two fingers in the air, and before Xaviara could take another breath, they were propelling Gloria out of the bridge and toward the brig.

Chapter 12

Nicholen was furious, but he kept his breathing even and counted the heartbeats pounding in his ears, using the technique he'd practiced to slow down his racing pulse. He stared at the empty doorway where his men and Gloria had disappeared. Anthony, the navigation officer, and Samantha, the communication officer, had their heads down and noses in their consoles. Xaviara was standing against a wall as though she wanted to blend into the grey and yellow background.

The only person he could trust anymore was her. "Come here."

Even her startled movement toward him was graceful. The surprised look that had taken over her gorgeous features was melting away with every step she took.

Damn, but she was poised, even under the most stressful of situations.

Tearing his eyes from her curvy form, he addressed the two human officers. "Will there be a problem following my orders?"

"No, sir," said Samantha first, followed quickly by Anthony's, "Absolutely not."

"Good." The two might find it odd he was addressing a diplomatic aide, but with the treachery he'd discovered, he didn't give a fuck. To Xaviara, he said, "Do you see what happened there?"

She nodded. "She should have found the transmission in the commdump."

"Yes, but it was also buried with a high level security code."

Xaviara's breathy gasp nearly made his desire spike, but his pounding heart rate had nearly slowed to its normal pace, and he was able to keep his body under control. Forebears, but she made all the discipline he'd practiced for years fly out the window with her mere presence.

"I've decrypted the rest of the message with your security clearance," said Samantha.

Nicholen kept himself from shifting uncomfortably again for another reason—he did not like that Camlan had insisted on updating their voice clearance to match the masquerade they were perpetuating. *There may come a time when you need to act on the* trincaar*'s authority*, Camlan had insisted. Nicholen regretted that it had finally come to this. "Play it."

Manda Aurellia's clear voice rang out over the speakers, all traces of static gone. "Begin. Anchor ship KH-159, this is lead ship KH-159. We have crashed-landed on alien planet UTP-8907. Engine failure. We require pick-up at the following coordinates." An artificial voice followed with the location. "Repeat."

Relief flooded him. With the coordinates confirmed from what the computer had displayed during the crash, it was a simple matter to fly into geosynchronous orbit and activate the matter transmitter. "Take us into the mesosphere, and prepare to mattrans them out of there."

"Sir," Anthony spoke up, "that will be impossible. We already tried to follow them on their crash route, but the planet's magnetic field is interfering with our navigation equipment that close to the surface."

Nicholen blinked. "What if—"

"Further," he continued, "even if I were to manually fly us into the correct orbit—and yes, I probably would be able to, given enough time—a field that dense would make it impossible unable to initiate safe mattrans."

Of course. If Nicholen wasn't so worked up over recent events, he would have put those two things together. "Are you saying we can't get them off the planet?"

"Not from where they're at now. I don't know about elsewhere."

"What do you mean you don't know about elsewhere? Isn't it your *job* to know about elsewhere?"

"I'll need more time, sir."

"Fine. Initiate a mapping of the region. I want to know if there's any location within a fifty kilometer radius that's safe to mattrans them. We'll worry about getting ourselves there later."

"Initiating. This will take some time."

"How much time?" The words came out sharper than he'd intended, but forebears, his *trincaar*'s life was on the line.

"For almost eight thousand square kilometers, eight hours."

Nicholen held in a sigh. "Do a life sign scan of one square kilometer as well. I want to know what they're dealing with down there."

"I'll need another hour for that."

It was already late, and nearly time for him—and probably Xaviara—to sleep. With Gloria off the bridge, Nicholen made another decision. "Go ahead. I'll be back in the morning to hear the results." He turned on his heel. "Oh, and Samantha?"

"Sir?" said the communication officer.

"Send a message down to tell them what we're doing. I'll leave it up to you to decide what to say, but don't mention the sabotage or arrest."

"Yes, sir."

* * *

Out in the hallway, Xaviara lifted her eyebrows and tried what she hoped came across as a coy smile. "So... Bedtime..."

The pained expression that had overtaken Nicholen's handsome features the moment he stepped onto the bridge melted into the lustful grin she'd seen after pleasuring him earlier. "Oh, sweet *viaar*, I would like nothing more than to fall into bed with you, but—"

He clamped his mouth shut as the kadyyza security guards who had dragged Gloria off toward the brig rounded the corner. The taller said, "We've secured your guest in the location you requested."

Euphemisms everywhere. At times, Xaviara found it laughable how much diplomats would dance around the real meaning behind words. Even a man who didn't believe himself diplomatic used them.

"Did she say anything?" Nicholen's pained expression was back.

"She insists she's not the saboteur."

"Of course she does."

"We questioned her but she gave us no information."

Nicholen nodded crisply. "I'll try in the morning. I believe the two of you are on duty for the next," his eyes flicked upward to check the time in his link, "ten hours?"

"Yes, sir."

"Good. Don't speak to her. Wait and see if she reveals anything. I'll ask for a full report in the morning."

Both saluted simultaneously and disappeared around the corner.

Xaviara jumped at her chance to try convincing Nicholen to drop whatever excuse he'd been about to formulate. She stepped forward and put her arms around his waist. When she tipped up her head to kiss him, his lips were soon on hers, his manhood stirring against her pelvis. Wetness pooled in her core as his tongue danced around her mouth.

But then he pulled back. "The first thing I learned in the military is how important sleep is for clear and rational decision-making."

Xaviara let out a small moan.

His erection stirred again. "Don't tempt me, *viaar.*" With a deft move, he extricated himself from her arms. "I would love to repay you for what you did earlier, but we need to get through this crisis first. I'll breathe much easier once we know your Manda and my Camlan are on their way to safety."

"All right." What more was there to do but agree? "You have an excellent point." Besides, they needed to stop canoodling in the hallway. All the excitement was making her take risks.

"We'll pick this up soon. I promise." He gave her a tiny push in the direction of her bunk. "Sleep well. And no trying to sneak into my room at night. I sleep naked."

His wink sent shivers of desire through her body. Sadly, she headed down the corridor in the opposite direction he was going.

Chapter 13

Xaviara was having the sexiest dream of her life. She was naked and bracing herself against the wall opposite Nicholen's bed while he thrust in and out, whispering flowing words in his own language. His fingers pressed into her hipbone, his cock was thick and hard, and her entire being shuddered with the force of their lovemaking.

She awoke to the dinging of her link, panties soaked through and sheets tangled between her legs. It took a second chirp before she figured out she was *not* screwing the hottest male alive. She activated her link. "Yes?"

"It's Nicholen. I have the results of the scan from the planet."

"Give me a minute." The words came out a croak.

"How about I meet you in the library in a few?" He sounded amused. Could he read her emotions through the link? Her heart was still pounding, and when she let out a breath, she moaned with the desire still pooling in her nether regions.

"Sounds fine." She ended the call before she could embarrass herself further.

The shared washroom down the hall had barely room for a mirror, sink, and shower, so she sat on the closed toilet lid while she brushed her teeth. She'd saved her water rations from yesterday, so she decided a quick rinse would calm her down. The shower itself was so tiny, she tried to imagine both herself and Nicholen inside together but failed—which somehow managed to push her raging libido down deep inside her.

She definitely would have to see about him paying her back today. Pleasuring a man had never made her this... this... *randy* before. But oh, how hot he was, sliding between her lips—

No, stop it! You'll spend the entire day in agony if you don't quit.

As she dried off, she thought about abandoned terraforming projects and all manner of beasts that could have evolved from the chemicals and radiation they'd doused the planet with a thousand years ago. *That* got her mind onto other things that made her heart race. *Poor Manda.* But her friend and superior was resourceful. *I'm sure she'll be fine.*

With combed hair, a fresh standard-issue uniform, and her tablet under one arm, Xaviara marched toward the library. She passed by a viewport that displayed the vibrant green planet. Deep blue ocean faded into the half of the planet bathed in darkness. The view was breathtaking.

The colors were even brighter than she remembered from yesterday.

Nicholen was alone inside, bending over a console displaying readouts from the lead ship. The sight of his broad shoulders and curve of his delectable buttocks made her stop in her tracks before she closed the door. *I could look at* this *view all day.*

"Good morning." She tried not to wonder what emotions he was getting from her now. "What's it look like down there?"

His grin was the same mischievous one from last night when she'd tried to entice him into coming to bed with her. Her cheeks heated. "Manda and Camlan are doing fine. The air is breathable, and we found a spot about thirty kilometers from where they crashed where it should be safe to mattrans them off the planet." He pointed to a topographical map. "Now they just need to get there."

"What about indigenous life?"

He pulled up more readings, which included sketches. "Plants. Lots and lots of plants. There are some reptile- and mammal-like creatures, but nothing larger than a small rodent."

She let out a breath. "Good."

Nicholen embraced her, and the heat of his body seared into her skin. "They'll be fine. Don't worry. I've got it under control."

Her stomach churned—of course he did. He let go, removing his delicious heat and muscled chest.

"Are you ready?" he asked softly.

"Ready for what?" Xaviara steadied herself, hoping she looked casual and not like she was about to swoon in his arms.

"Ready for questioning Gloria? I need you to watch from your room again. You can make observations I can't."

"Of course." This secret meeting in the library made her pulse race. "Give me five minutes." She reached up to press his link and activate a call to her own, brushing her fingers across his ear and over the scar on his cheek.

He tucked his tablet under his arm, kissed her, and scooted her out the door.

Once back in her room, she pulled up the feed into the brig. Nicholen's face was visible through the doorway. "I'm ready," she said into her link.

He pushed the door open button and sauntered into the brig. A beep signaled the connection between herself and Nicholen had moved to ship-only—all quanten connectivity stopped at the door to prevent prisoners from communicating with the outside galaxy.

Gloria was sitting on the pallet, back against the beige wall, paging through her tablet in the languorous manner of someone reading a magazine. She must have downloaded it before being hauled in here. One more page flip, and she stood, setting the tablet on the small indentation that served as a night stand. She kissed her fingers and held them out in the traditional kadyyza greeting, though she didn't move close enough to allow Nicholen to kiss them in return. "Good day, *trincaar*. How may I serve?"

Nicholen's jaw took a hard line as he clenched it. He stepped forward, placed, his hands behind his back, and spread his leg in a stance that looked pure military—and pure *sexy*—to Xaviara. "We have some things to discuss."

"Indeed." She inclined her head.

* * *

Nicholen drew out the silence. Gloria was a seasoned diplomat, one unlikely to cave to the pressure of dead air, but she was also in a disadvantaged position, what with being behind bars. Her emotions wafted toward him like a spicy perfume, not much different from what he'd picked up from her these past few days. She was holding her emotions in check, keeping herself calm.

He admired that.

The thought somehow distracted him, though, pulling his mind toward the sexy aide secretly watching him. Despite her youth and how early she was in her career, Xaviara was also poised. The only out-of-control emotion he'd sensed from her was the sultry smell of her lust, which reminded him of lush, beautiful flowers in full bloom.

That was enough silence. It was time for him to speak.

"Do you have any response to the charge of sabotage levied against you?" he said.

"Not guilty." Her emotions were steady, though the scent of rain-spattered earth churned underneath. Nerves, then, but that told him nothing. Everyone was nervous when accused, whether or not they had done it.

"That's a likely story." He inserted derision in his voice. Here was his forte: the interrogation. Diplomacy and parading around as a prince left him off-balance. But when it came to getting to the truth of a matter, he was in his element.

Gloria didn't answer. Smart. Maybe diplomacy and interrogations weren't so different from one another—but still, he disliked the pretense required by diplomatic negotiations.

He said, "You have the resources to cause a crash. You have the security clearance to bury their attempts at contact through the magnetic storm. And you have the motive for wanting to cause an intergalactic incident between our two species."

"Motive? What motive?"

"Your PDJ stock."

Gloria's eyebrows raised. "I don't know what you're talking about."

"You're lying." What did Xaviara think about this new side of him she was getting a glimpse of now? He could only hope it wouldn't scare her off. "Your emotions give you away. And I have the information right here." He flashed his tablet at her.

Gloria let out a breath. "You're right. I apologize. I..."

Now they were getting somewhere. She was flustered.

"I do own stock in PDJ Company, but I would *never* betray my integrity to sabotage a mission. Those two sides of me are separate. My financial situation is personal, and my job as Senior Ambassador is professional."

Interestingly enough, the spicy scent of her emotions was becoming stronger. This was something she cared about deeply. Her passion was fueling her calm. Nicholen had not expected this.

But he still had to dig.

"Where were you before the crash? Someone interrupted the ship-wide security footage."

"It wasn't me."

"Where were you before the crash?" he repeated.

"Catching up on reports in my bunk." The faintest of smirks appeared on Gloria's lips. "If you had matched the wiped footage with my security clearance, we wouldn't be having this conversation. In fact, I don't think you're confident you've caught the right saboteur. I think you made me wait all night to put me off guard, and now you're pressing for answers you don't have."

"So you have no alibi?"

"No, but I don't need one. I didn't do it." She took a step forward. "Let me help you find the saboteur... *trincaar*." She drew out the word.

She knows. Nicholen kept his face still, betrayed no emotion.

"I can help you find whoever did this," Gloria continued, "and it will be a much better use of our collective resources than keeping me penned up in this cell."

"What about the commdump? Explain to me how a seasoned Senior Ambassador—" he used the same inflection she had a moment ago "—failed to find the lead ship's message."

She blinked at him.

"I'm waiting."

"Could we please speak alone?"

Nicholen's lips tightened. "We are alone."

Gloria nodded toward his ear. "I know you have *some-one* listening in on the link. And," she lifted a chin toward the camera, "watching, I'm sure. I need to know this isn't going to leave this room."

If he cut off Xaviara's access, she would be upset at being excluded. However, his libido had to take a backseat to his duties—like Gloria claimed, he *did* separate his work and personal lives. At least, he usually did. It had been quite muddled ever since Xaviara had surprised him with the revelation that she was aware of he and Camlan's subterfuge.

He reached up and severed the link with Xaviara. Then he turned and pressed the red button below the camera, cutting off the last of the communication. She would understand this was the only way they would get the truth out of Gloria.

He spoke before she could. "How long have you known?"

"Known what, *trincaar*?" She smiled.

He waited.

She kept smiling.

He waited some more.

The smile slid off her face. "My memories of the prince match you," she said, "but I've been dealing with the kadyyza long enough to know that when something is off, it's due to your genetically enhanced abilities. And something is off about you, Nicholen. You're really the captain, and the man down there is the true *trincaar*. Is that right?"

He nodded curtly. It was the only thing he would give her.

She stepped forward and pressed her hands to the bars. "Then you need me more than ever. I'm not the one that sabotaged this mission. In fact, my career is on the line. Let me help you."

"Tell me why I should believe that."

Her emotions suddenly shifted; a scent like a torrential rainstorm smacked into him. He nearly reeled backward. She was afraid? Of what?

"Gloria," he said, "tell me."

"Fine." Her hands dropped. "I'll get right to it. I'm suffering from the early stages of a disease called Mayzar Syndrome."

"I'm sorry to hear that."

"It's a degenerative brain disease. Are you familiar with Alzheimer's?"

The translator didn't have a kadyyza word for it, and the English word came out harsh and ugly. Nicholen shook his head.

"It was a disease that was mostly cured a long time ago. Tests are done in utero and treatment applied early on, like with all the other diseases we've eliminated. However, one strain can be detected but not cured until it manifests itself. I have it. It's manifested itself."

He tried to be delicate but couldn't find the words. "How are you still acting in your current capacity?"

"I'm being treated. That's part of this whole thing. In order to treat it, it must appear. Once it appears, I lose some of my implicit memories. Treatment is underway, but I never know what is going to be there and what's not. I forgot about the commdump. *Forgot.*" She sounded so bitter, he couldn't muster up suspicion.

"But why not take time off?" he pressed.

The rainstorm scent grew stronger. "I haven't told anyone outside my medical team."

He was stunned into silence.

"You know how the Coalition is. Ambassadors have to be seen as intelligent. Mentally nimble. I can't risk word of this getting out, especially since the treatment only takes about six months."

"But what about your staff? Why not bring someone senior in to make sure these mistakes don't happen? Why bring in all young staff?"

She laughed a bitter laugh. "Someone senior would know right away that there's something wrong with me. They would be *obligated* to file a report."

He crossed his arms. "And you think I'm not?"

"Whatever you decide to do, this brig is a terrible place for me to be. The fact alone that I'm in here might mean an intergalactic incident, even if we get your prince off the surface safely." She stepped back, took a deep breath, and let her shoulders relax. The rain scent disappeared. "Here's what I suggest: leave me in here. Think about alternative suspects. Check into them. If it *is* me, I can't do any more harm. My link isn't working, and your security guards are quite fastidious—no one's getting to me."

"Let me see your tablet."

She crossed the room, picked it up, and hurried back to hand it to him. He inspected it.

"You're right."

He handed it back to her.

"Well?" she asked.

"I'll think on your advice," Nicholen said. He was convinced, but he needed some time to review the other two suspects. With Gloria eliminated, that left only two other people, Breniel and Lianndra—and both were kadyyza. Neither seemed capable, and he didn't like admitting that one of his own kind could do such a thing to their *trincaar*. Maybe Xaviara's algorithm had picked up something more amongst the humans.

"Thank you," said Gloria.

Her eyes followed him as he turned and left.

Chapter 14

Xaviara chewed her lip as she stared at the blank screen. Nicholen had barely hesitated when Gloria asked him to shut down the feed. What was she saying to him that she didn't want a junior member of her staff to hear? Was it a confession? Was it something about Xaviara herself? No, that would be ridiculous.

Xaviara's tablet beeped.

Worries churning through her mind, Xaviara swiped it open, glad for the distraction. Gloria couldn't possibly be telling Nicholen something that would turn him against her—what would that even be?—but she couldn't shake the feeling that something was off.

As she scrolled through the information displayed from her search algorithm of the rest of the human staff, she inwardly groaned. Another suspect, one that was looking even more promising than Gloria: Piotr, her rival.

As much as she didn't like him, she didn't want him to be behind betraying their entire species. The sinking feeling in her stomach amplified as she read through the information. She keyed in a few phrases, delving deeper into the details provided. *Oh, yes. This makes sense.*

Whatever Gloria was telling Nicholen was moot now. It seemed that they had a new prime suspect.

Her link beeped. "Meet me in the library," said Nicholen. The library—not her quarters. What could it mean?

Nicholen was waiting for her when she arrived and shut the door.

"Um..." she started, hating herself for being so hesitant. This strong man needed a match that was just as confident as he was. She tried again. "My search uncovered a new suspect."

He seemed far away. She couldn't read the expression on his face—one part determination, one part frustration, and one part something else.

"What happened in there?" she asked.

"I can't tell you."

Although she suspected that response, the words were like a slap in the face. "Oh."

His expression softened. Was he reading her emotions? That was so *annoying*.

"It's fine, I understand," she said.

"For Camlan's safety, I'm obligated not to reveal what Gloria told me."

"We've both shared things we shouldn't." The words came out of Xaviara's mouth more shrill than she would have liked.

"Yes, but..." And now the expression was one of a man digging himself into a deeper hole. *Men. The same whether they're human or kadyyza.* He seemed to be floundering and then he pulled himself tall. Despite herself, lust raged inside Xaviara for this sexy man. "I can't. I'm sorry."

"Fine. I'm here to serve the delegation, after all." The words rang hollow, even if they were true. "Do you want to know what I've found?"

"Tell me."

This was a Nicholen she didn't know. His face was neutral, closed off, his lips pinched. All signs of the playfulness of earlier were gone. Whatever had happened in there was serious. "I have a new suspect. A better suspect. A *much* better suspect."

"Out with it."

His abruptness stung again. "It's Piotr, one of my fellow aides." She was both dismayed and delighted to have discovered it, given the ridiculous rivalry that had gotten her in trouble on the space station. Was that only a couple days ago? So much had happened. "But that's not his real name. His real name is Viktor Lukin. I found evidence of motive. And I checked some facts about his background that I'd nearly forgotten. He definitely knows how to hack into the main computer system and hide the commdump information."

Nicholen's face didn't change. He stared at the wall behind her.

"His older brother was killed during the Day of Darkness. And that tattoo you might have seen on his wrist, the
circle with the infinity inside? That's a symbol of an elite
fraternity of computer hackers he joined in university, the
Incongruous."

* * *

Damn it. Things seemed to be going sideways now.
Just twelve hours ago, Nicholen was confident that he'd
found the saboteur, and now, not only was he wrong, but a
new lead had cropped up. Still, it wasn't any more promising than the others they still had on the list—Lianndra
and Breniel were still in the running with Gloria no longer
looking guilty. He absolutely believed her story. Emotions
didn't lie.

And clearly Xaviara was upset with him over hiding
what Gloria had to say. He didn't blame her, but he'd
made a promise to keep the woman's secret.

"Why did Piotr change his name?"

Xaviara's emotions were all over the place—the same
floral scent of arousal wafted from her, but it was now
masked now by a metallic tang of hurt. "It's human cus-
tom to change our given names if we become famous, to
blend in and live a normal life. He's not famous, but his
brother was for leading the counterattack against the
kadyyza."

She was looking at the tablet, flicking through information. Inside his link, Nicholen pulled open the snap of
the mail she'd sent him. *^V@GK@L^ Preparations
^V@GK@L^ complete. ^V@GK@L^* read the first line.
Things were starting to fall into place.

She finished, "I don't know for sure, but that has to be it. Every human knows the name of Damien Lukin."

Nicholen nodded once. He'd slipped into military mode again. Too much was coming at him to relax into the calm, swaggering, princely figure that Camlan wanted him to be. He took a long breath in through his nose and released it through his mouth.

Not working.

He looked down at Xaviara.

Her long hair shone under the lights of the library. Her lips were puckered, likely in annoyance at him. He wanted to kiss her... and so he did. Stepping forward, he placed a hand on her chin and lifted her face toward his. The touch of her soft lips was electric. He slid her mouth open with his tongue and found hers. She battled with him, pressing herself into his mouth—and now he was hard again. *Forebears, but this woman is fantastic.*

Then she pushed him away and drew back. "We don't have time for this." The metallic scent of hurt was stronger now. What had he done wrong? The kiss was supposed to be an apology for his abruptness earlier, but obviously it had made things worse. She needed to understand that he had to keep some secrets. Didn't she?

"I—"

"Let's go see what's happening on the bridge." Her tone was clipped. "And then go question Piotr. See if he had the opportunity."

His erection was settling down again. Good thing, since she was right.

Before he could answer, she pressed the door open button and gracefully glided into the corridor. He could do nothing but follow, trying not to watch the sway of her hips, which had taken on a decidedly more antagonistic rhythm.

He let her go into the bridge first, counted to fifty, and opened the door. Xaviara was making smalltalk with Anthony. One eye on her, he said, "Report," to Samantha.

"Sir," she said, "the saboteur struck again."

Nicholen's lower lip twitched, his only tell for high-stress situations. After all this time, it was the one thing he couldn't control about himself. "Why wasn't I notified?"

"I dealt with it," she said. Impressive, since as Gloria had confirmed, all the humans were junior staff. "My outgoing message was routed from the standard emergency frequency to a lesser used channel—not canceled, because I would have detected that right away."

"A clever way of keeping you from knowing what had been done."

"Yes, but I was prepared for something like that, sir, so I was watching for it."

Nicholen decided that he liked this woman. "And your message made it to the planet?"

"Yes, the party below is on their way to the rendezvous location as we speak."

Finally, something was going well. "Good. Anything else?"

"Yes. Some of their emergency supplies were destroyed in the crash. They only have enough food for two days.

Fortunately, they should arrive by then, if they don't run into any unforeseen circumstances."

He held in a grunt of frustration. So much for things going well. Unforeseen circumstances seemed to be the theme of this trip.

"I'm monitoring their communications on all frequencies. I picked up some static a while back, but the magnetic field is strong and still interfering."

"It's not going to abate," said Xaviara. "We just have to trust they'll be there in good time."

"Agreed," said Samantha.

"Thank you," said Nicholen. "Continue the monitoring and call me if anything changes. How long until they arrive?"

"If all goes well, it'll be twenty-four to thirty-six hours. The terrain is prairie first, and then jungle and beach-like conditions. It would be faster to go through the jungle, but if it turns out to be unnavigable, it'll be better for them to go along the shoreline."

"Then tomorrow, we'll be in a position to rescue them."

"Yes, sir."

The newest interference meant Gloria couldn't be behind the sabotage. Even if she was, she had an accomplice on the outside, a dangerous, well-equipped accomplice who would be poised to strike once more when they mounted the rescue.

Fuck. He was tempted to throw the entire crew into the brig and rescue his prince without the aid of anyone.

Nicholen lifted an eyebrow at Xaviara and tilted his head toward the door.

Chapter 15

Nicholen was jumping all over the place, and Xaviara could barely keep up. He led the way, and she
couldn't help but allow her eyes to rove to that
delectable ass, in tight, fine shape from whatever training
he did to keep himself in peak condition. Those strong
legs, the curve of his back.

She matched him stride for stride, even though she had
to push herself to keep up through the hallway. And a
good thing, too. After that kiss, she wanted nothing more
than to throw herself at him, but she was also upset.

She had to remember that.

Under her breath, she said, "You can't just kiss me and
think that's going to fix anything."

"I didn't—" He stopped his purposeful march. "It's not
that. It's..."

"It's what?"

"I needed to focus. Kissing you calmed me." He started walking again.

She blinked and scurried to keep up. "Oh." This changed things, but only a little. "That's still not how you treat people. You and I need to figure out what's going on between us, and this isn't the way to do it."

"I agree," he said. They were at the door to Piotr's bunk. "Do you want to continue this conversation in the hall?"

"No, of course not."

"Then let's table it for later." He lifted a hand to push the doorbell.

"What are you doing?"

His finger was on the button. "What do you mean?"

"Shouldn't I go back to my bunk?"

"No. This isn't working. I need you here, in person."

"I'm just a junior aide." His assertion seemed more than just a declaration of needing her help, though. It seemed he was saying...

"That doesn't matter." Nicholen's hand moved from the doorbell to her shoulder. His touch was like fire—a good fire, raging through her. "You're smart and focused, and I want you in there with me. I don't know this person, but you do."

Uh-oh. Of all the suspects to choose to need her for, Piotr was the absolute wrong one. But what could she say? "Piotr and I don't exactly get along."

"Then you won't put up with any bullshit from him. Right?"

"I suppose." Should she tell him what had happened before the kadyyza delegation had arrived?

Before she could decide, Nicholen pushed the doorbell.

"Who is it?" came Piotr's voice.

"Valkkh Nicholen, *trincaar* of the Imdali System."

A thump, and then the door slid open. Eyes wide, Piotr filled the doorway, obviously blocking their view of his bunk. Xaviara tipped her head to the side, curious at what he was hiding. He glared and moved in front of her. Before he did, she caught a glimpse of the ship's mainframe up on his console.

"Can I help you?" said Piotr, still staring at Xaviara.

"We have some questions. Please come with us." Nicholen held out a hand, the perfect image of a prince of a solar system. His cape flapped behind him. He might not think he represented Imdali well, but Xaviara had a different opinion.

Silent, Piotr hurried into the hall, slammed the door close button, and pressed his thumb to the locking mechanism before Xaviara could get another look at his console. Nicholen turned on a heel and led the way. Xaviara smiled at Piotr until he huffed and stomped off down the hall.

"What were you working on?" She kept her voice neutral, knowing the question itself would be enough to needle him.

"None of your damn business." He glanced at Nicholen. "Pardon me, *trincaar*."

Nicholen grunted. "We're going to the ready room." Probably a better place than the library for an interrogation. Xaviara was pleased—she didn't want her memories from there sullied by Piotr's bad attitude.

They went through the bridge and into the ready room. Samantha was still hard at work, poring over the commdump files. On another console, the report for attempted communications scrolled.

Once they were inside, the door shut behind the three of them, and Nicholen gestured to a chair. "Please sit."

* * *

Piotr's eyebrows lifted, but he sat anyway, right on the edge of the chair, looking like he would jump up at any moment. *Good, stay off-balance*, thought Nicholen. Xaviara stood at his elbow, and he loved her strong, sultry presence next to him. A small part of him hoped she would be impressed with how he conducted the interrogation. She wasn't able to see how he'd finished the discussion with Gloria, and he still regretted that he had to keep information from her.

He decided to start in a different place than with Gloria. Someone had gained access to the lead ship before they left Sol Alliance Space Station 47, in order to access the mu-drive and create the problem Breniel had described. "Where were you two nights ago?"

Piotr blinked. "The night before we left the space station?"

"Yes."

"In my bunk. Sleeping."

"All night?"

"Yes, all night." Piotr dropped his eyes and then raised them again, as if he realized how guilty it was making him look. "I mean, that is to say, I got there after we finished dinner with your delegation, and I watched a movie, and then I went to bed."

"He's lying. And I don't like being lied to." Another tactic, one of his favorite. Talk about them like they're not in the room, and it makes their blood boil. "Do you regularly lie to the leadership in the delegations you're assigned to?"

"I'm... I didn't..." Piotr stammered, shifting.

The metallic scent from Xaviara was back and stronger than ever. Thank the forebears, though, it didn't seem to be directed at Nicholen this time. "What were you working on when we came to get you, Piotr?" she demanded. "I saw what you had up on the screen. You have no reason to be in the computer's inner systems."

He jumped up. "It's none of your damn business!"

Nicholen folded his arms and shifted his stance so he was standing with feet shoulder-width apart. He took a full two second count to do so, and Piotr stepped backward, bumped into the chair, and sat down hard. He was acting guilty, all right, but Nicholen knew from previous experience that didn't mean he was guilty about what they expected.

"What's the matter, Piotr? Is there something you don't want us to know?" said Xaviara.

Forebears, but she was forceful when she wanted to be. He loved seeing her at work. He would have loved to let her conduct the entire interrogation, but it was important that Piotr saw him as in charge.

"What's this about?" Now Piotr was looking back and forth between the two of them. "Why are *you* working with *him*?"

Nicholen held up a hand before Xaviara could answer. "Not your concern," he growled. Rivalry, indeed. Clearly, there was no love lost between these two.

"I..." Piotr shrank in the chair.

Nicholen waited, hand still raised.

"Why do you want to know?" Piotr said meekly.

Nicholen considered and then decided to take a gamble. Whatever this man was hiding, it wasn't anything nefarious. He was acting embarrassed, not guilty. "We believe that someone sabotaged the lead ship. You were our prime suspect."

Piotr's mouth dropped open. "I *was?*"

"You have motive and means. And if I wanted to, I could confirm opportunity. But I'm starting to wonder..."

If he'd been guilty, he would have looked smug, but instead, Piotr only looked crestfallen. "I'm sorry you'd think that of me. But no, I didn't do it."

"But what about your brother?" interjected Xaviara, glancing toward Nicholen. The metallic tang was back. She was annoyed again.

"My... ? Oh." Piotr looked at his hands. "You know my real name."

"Yes, we do, Viktor," said Nicholen.

Piotr heaved a sigh. "That was a long time ago. I grieved and now I'm over it. Are you really going to make me tell you what I was doing?"

"Yes," they both said at the same time, but it was Xaviara Piotr was looking at.

He looked so miserable Nicholen almost asked her to leave the room so he could get this poor guy to spill his secrets. But after the Gloria debacle, he needed to tread carefully.

"Fine." Piotr sighed again. "Fine, *fine*. Anthony and I are having an affair."

"What now?" exclaimed Xaviara. "Navigation officer Anthony?"

"Fraternization within ambassadorial teams is frowned upon, especially between junior and senior members." Piotr looked to Nicholen with this explanation. "We're not technically allowed to be dating without declaring it. But I don't know if we're dating. We're definitely..." He colored. "It's complicated. Anyway. I was erasing some of the footage of what we did last night in his bunk."

"And the night before we left, you were with him."

"We *were* watching movies!" Piotr exclaimed, looking miserable, shoulders hunched and brow furrowed.

"Get up," said Nicholen. "Show us the footage."

Piotr leapt to his feet. "What?"

"I believe you, but I need to see it for myself." Trust, then verify. It applied to his own team primarily, but he should extend the same courtesy to the human team.

"Do I have to?"

"Just enough to prove that what you're saying is true."

"Yeah," said Xaviara. "We don't need to see all... that." Her waving hand gesture in Piotr's direction said enough.

"All right," he said. "Come with me."

Chapter 16

"Well, that was a bust," said Xaviara. They were back in the library, going over the clues they'd assembled. She'd been tempted to suggest going back to her bunk, but at Nicholen's direction, this was where they'd ended up. And a good thing, too, since she wanted to put her hands all over this man. The library afforded them a little privacy—but not too much.

"Yes," agreed Nicholen, "I would have preferred not to see Anthony's bare ass."

She laughed. That's where Piotr had stopped the video right before they'd arrived. "Yeah, I could have done without that, too."

Nicholen's violet eyes were luminous in the lower light of the library. Perhaps this room was a bit more private than they needed right now. She ached to press her lips to his again. From the way he kept looking at her lips, he was thinking the same thing. The sexy look from before came over his face. Hooded eyes, slight smirk.

He moved closer, leaning forward in the chair. *He's going to kiss me, and I'm going to let him, and time is going to slip away.* Xaviara had to say something to halt all of this at once, so they could finish the task at hand. Manda's life was on the line.

"You know this is never going to work." *Oh, shit, too harsh, too harsh!*

Nicholen drew back. "What?"

"You and me. You're a Captain of the Royal Guard. I'm just an aide." As she said it, she realized it was true. What could he possibly want with her? "And we live light-years apart."

"I thought we'd figure it out when the mission was over."

"Yes, we can try, but honestly, how?" What was she *doing?* She liked this man, as infuriating as he was. And, promised payback aside, she was more attracted to him than anyone in a long time. But she had to stop this back and forth. She needed to know if he, too, was serious. They could sleep together—she was fine with that—but she wanted to know if it was going to be something more.

"There's the spaceway," he said. As part of this accord, the Imdali and Sol governments were negotiating setting up high-speed relay points between their two systems. The two-day journey they were on would be cut down to about eight hours.

"That's still months away, and only if the treaty is successful," she pressed.

"In the meantime, there are holocalls and mail."

He seemed to be serious. "True, but what—"

"Wait," he said. "Mail."

"Long distance stuff is tough."

He held up a hand. "It is, but that's not what I mean. We need to come back to this conversation, little *viaar*."

His use of the nickname melted her again. It was so... so... *sexy*.

"Let's pull up that mail from your date with Boring Tom," he said. "I want to look at it. I think I just figured out who our saboteur is."

* * *

The mail was the key. Nicholen was sure of it.

*^V@GK@L^ Preparations ^V@GK@L^ complete. ^V@GK@L^*

*^V@GK@L^ Operation Mallard ^V@GK@L^ Duck confirmed. ^V@GK@L^*

*^V@GK@L^ Negotiation team arrives ^V@GK@L^ tomorrow 22:00. ^V@GK@L^*

*^V@GK@L^ Attach previously provided packages to lead ship per ^V@GK@L^ schematics. Be prepared to receive further instructions. ^V@GK@L^*

*^V@GK@L^ First payment initiated ^V@GK@L^ to account on file. ^V@GK@L^*

As the mail splashed across Xaviara's tablet, he nodded.

"I think I know who it is, too. Let's check one more thing," she said and logged into the ship's computer. "Too much has been happening too fast."

He wasn't sure if she was referring to the situation on the ship or their relationship. Maybe it was both. Forebears, but he ached for this woman. Her lithe fingers keyed their way to the commdump and scrolled back to the recent archives.

Clever. They'd been so busy, they hadn't yet checked the one thing that confirmed their suspicions.

"I usually have to check the reference manual when I'm looking through this thing," said Xaviara, "but I think this is what we're looking for, yes?" She turned the tablet to Nicholen.

His eyes jumped down the page. At the time when the sabotage was taking place, Breniel was actively running diagnostics on the engine. The saboteur may have covered their tracks by knocking out the ship-wide security feed when implementing the sabotage, but he or she didn't think to cloud the other suspects' activities.

"Breniel didn't do it," Xaviara and Nicholen said in unison.

"That leaves Viktor and Lianndra," he said. "I'm certain Gloria didn't do it, either."

"The key is in what we thought was garbage." Her eyes flickered across the tablet, taking in the mail again. "That's not actually garbage; it's a security encryption. For some reason, his mail software didn't filter it into the form of a signature. It appeared as gobbledegook."

"Yes," breathed Nicholen.

Xaviara raised her eyes to his, and sparks flew between them. Her gaze was intense, the same as it had been when she was going down on him. Fuck, but he wanted to make her look like that again... and again... and again...

After this was all over, he would.

"VL," she said. "Those are Viktor Lukin's initials."

He nodded. "But..."

"But they're also Lianndra Verrytto's backward. Except it's not backward. Your people go by surname first and given name second. VL. Verrytto Lianndra."

Her brilliant mind had arrived at the same spot that his had nearly in record time. She was his match, in mind and body both. However this thing played out, he had to make this work with her. Rules be damned, they would be together, no matter what.

"And," she continued, the same intense expression making it very difficult for him to concentrate on her words, "the middle letters are GK. *Geshhina Kadyyza*, or 'Kadyyza Forever.'"

The translator let him hear her sexy accent glide over the words in his native language. The literal translation was indeed "Kadyyza Forever," but it meant so much more. The *Geshhina Kadyyza* were a terrorist organization, the ones the royal family suspected were behind the eldest brother Willex's death.

They used the letters as a call to action. Kadyyza Forever—but also standing *above* all others, with no foes nor friends as equals. They were a supremacist group, one who opposed any and all alliances with outside species.

"I've heard of them," she whispered. "They're awful. Assassinations. Spaceship sabotage. You were right about Lianndra."

"This is one thing I don't like being vindicated in," he answered.

This time, the metallic scent coming from Xaviara had a tinge of sweetness to it. She was hurt again, but not at him. She was, instead, hurt on his behalf.

"Oh, Nicholen," she said softly. "I'm sorry."

Normally, he would have stiffened his spine, stepped back, and unleashed a biting remark. But this time, her tender sadness for him was...

Nice.

"Thank you."

The tablet dropped to her side, and she stepped forward to kiss him. Her lips were as soft as the floral scent of arousal wafting like a heady ambrosia from her skin. He hesitated a moment and then plunged in full force to the kiss.

* * *

Xaviara met his lust in kind, pressing back against his roving tongue. He slid his hands down her back, then gripped her ass. As her nipples blossomed under the restraining uniform, she felt his manhood surge again. Grabbing her by the hips, Nicholen sat down abruptly in one of the library chairs and pulled her into his lap. Fully clothed, he squeezed her against himself, and she reveled in the feel of his member rubbing against the cleft between her legs.

She wanted more. She wanted so much more.

"We're in the library," she gasped. "Maybe we should—"

He captured her earlobe in his mouth and reached out a hand to slap the lock mechanism on the door.

"Authorization code required," said the computer.

She squirmed as he let his teeth scrape over her earlobe. "Do you want me to stop?" His hands paused on her backside.

"No," she gasped. "Don't stop."

"Door lock authorized by *Trincaar* Valkkh Nicholen."

The door lock mechanism purred.

He buried his face in her breasts, pulling first one free and then the other. His tongue found her left nipple, and she suppressed a cry of pleasure. He tongued her, swirling first clockwise, then counterclockwise. "Fuck, you're beautiful." He pulled back to admire the glistening tip before sucking her right bud into her mouth.

Shocks of pleasure shot through Xaviara's belly to bury deep inside her.

One of his hands roved over her torso to the front. Nicholen clamped her against his hips, thrusting with his fully clothed member against her pleasure center. *How did he find it?* And then she realized, *His psy-sense.*

Her body flamed with the realization. What must it be like for him?

His thumb worked its way into her standard-issue dress pants. She worked them free to hang off one leg, and he lifted her to adjust his rock-hard member over her panty-clad entrance. She gasped as she slammed against him, and he ground himself into her. His thumb found her nub and made a lazy circle that sent liquid hot desire surging through her body.

Finding a rhythm, she rode his fully clothed shaft. Slickness coated the inside of her panties, and she moaned against his chest. As if that were a cue, he captured her mouth with his. His left hand was everywhere—her buttocks, her back, her thigh—and his right hand was strumming a rhythm on her love button that was sending her sky high.

"Oh, God, Nicholen," she moaned against his mouth.

He pulled away to purr in her ear. "Yes, my little *viaar*, come for me."

She sucked in a breath, relaxing as his thumb worked its magic and his cock lifted her higher into the realms of ecstasy. With a cry, she complied, gripping his shoulders and clamping her thighs around his. Wave after wave flowed over her, and the room went hazy. His thumb stilled, pressing against her.

Finally, she relaxed and stilled and slumped against his body.

His member throbbed beneath her.

Pulling back, she said, "Let me—"

He interrupted. "That was part one of your payback."

She grinned, feeling a little giddy and silly and definitely satisfied—for the moment. His answering grin made her stomach flop in a delicious way.

He held her against him, even when she tried to pull away. Giggling, she kissed him again. Finally, he said, "We should go."

All the unsaid words hung in the air between them, but for now, Xaviara was content to let them go. "You're right."

Reluctantly, she attempted to stand once more and he released her. When she wobbled, he caught her hand in his. "Need help?"

"I'm good."

Grinning, she straightened her uniform and swung a leg over the chair to stand next to him. She tugged at her rumpled pants, pulling them back over her leg.

"I'll just need a minute," he said, erection still apparent.

"Do you need me to turn around?" she teased.

"Your fine ass isn't going to help matters."

"Well, hurry up, we've got a job to do."

When he winked, she had to grip the chair to keep from going weak in the knees.

Chapter 17

orebears, but Xaviara's hot. She was soft as a summer breeze and sharp as a knife's edge. Her compassion stoked something deep inside him, something he thought didn't even exist. He thought he was happy focusing on his career and protecting his prince, but now he wanted to protect someone else.

A mate.

He wanted nothing more than to throw away his self-restraint and bury himself inside her, but they needed to worry about Lianndra right now. Besides, he was serious about pursuing a relationship with her, even if she seemed hesitant. Once this was all over, once Camlan and Manda were safe, they would sit down and have a long talk. Maybe fully clothed, maybe not. Either way, he would make his feelings clear and show her how committed he was to attempting a long-distance relationship.

Thinking about the more serious side of things calmed his raging erection. He closed his eyes, took a deep breath, and opened them.

Xaviara was grinning at him. "I love that I can get to you like that."

"I love it, too." Now under control, he said, "Unlock the door," to the ship's AI.

"What next?" said Xaviara, her face falling from its mischievous grin into the concerned expression she'd worn when they were sorting through their suspects. She picked up her tablet, abandoned on one of the keyboard ledges, and ran a thumb along an edge.

"We haul her into the brig and interrogate her until she cracks." Nicholen pressed his link. "Security team, find Lianndra Verrytto and bring her into custody."

"She thought stirring up your rivalry will throw you off the trail."

He nodded. "She'll have set something up to sabotage the rescue attempt. This organization is not known for mercy. They take no prisoners, and the *trincaar* has probably been on their hit list for years. It's a wonder she waited so long."

"Opportunity," Xaviara said. "She's probably been waiting for years to have the perfect setup, and our delegation was just that."

"Yes, makes sense." His link beeped.

His second-in-command's voice came through. "Lianndra isn't in her bunk. We've searched the public areas, but she's nowhere."

"What?" Nicholen's pulse raced. "Find her!" To Xaviara, he said, "She's disappeared."

She frowned. "Figures, but this ship is only so big, right? It's only a matter of time. What are we going to do while they look?"

"I have an idea," he said. "We're going to recruit Piotr to hack into her console and stop whatever she's planning, before she can strand Manda and Camlan on the planet forever."

"Oh, boy," she said. "Good luck to us."

* * *

"Why should I help you?" demanded Piotr.

Xaviara wanted to strangle him yet again, but she held her irritation in check. They were locked in the library. "You have *got* to be kidding me. You're a member of this delegation. It's your *duty*—"

"You accused me of being a traitor!"

She sighed.

Nicholen sat in the chair to her left, the same place they'd, well, humped. Such an indelicate, immature word, but there was little else she could use to describe it, and the mere thought of it gave her goosebumps. He glanced over, a smile playing across his lips—*oh, no, he's reading me again*—but that only served to make her goosebumps get goosebumps. She clenched muscles deep inside herself to quell the rising desire.

"Are you really telling me that you'd leave the head of this delegation and your boss stranded down there? Does the life of the Captain of the Royal Guard mean so little to you?" said Xaviara. They'd opted not to reveal Nicholen's true identity to Piotr. Keeping his secret seemed the prudent thing to do until they had no choice.

Piotr blinked and then blinked again, a nervous habit he'd have to quash before he could lead his own delegation. Xaviara prided herself on noticing these details: he was close to cracking.

"You know not helping us is a punishable offense," she said. "You'll go to prison."

"*Fine!*" He spat the word. "You don't have to threaten me. I'll help you. But you didn't have to be such an ass kisser in front of the prince earlier."

Nicholen, prudently, stayed silent.

"I wasn't being an ass kisser." She kept her voice even. "Nicholen asked for my help in finding the saboteur, as Manda's second-in-command."

Piotr tsked loudly. It was a wonder he didn't roll his eyes. "Second-in-command, my eye. First of all, we're both aides. Second of all, you're an ass kisser with her, too."

"I can't help that I take pride in my job!"

"Like I don't?"

"You're the one that inserted that video in my presentation!"

"You're the one that dumped coffee on me!"

Xaviara's cheeks heated. He'd spilled the secret of her immature behavior in front of the man whom she was hoping would become her lover. She and Piotr glared at one another, and she took in a deep breath. *Calm down.*

"I appreciate the chance to see the inner workings of the human delegation,. It's nice to know that the kadyyza aren't the only ones with hidden rivalries..." said Nicholen.

Xaviara would have laughed if she wasn't so irritated.

"... but we have a job to do. Are you going to help us or not, Piotr?"

"I said I would."

"Don't sulk." Xaviara couldn't help but get the jab in. "We came to you because we needed someone with your expertise."

Piotr snorted. "Don't flatter me."

"We're not," interjected Nicholen. "I have a duty to protect my people, which includes those under my care in this delegation. If you weren't the right man for the job, I'd go to the one who was."

Piotr's lips twitched. He was suppressing a smile. "Thank you. It means a lot." *Don't flatter him, indeed.* "Yes, of course I'll help. Tell me, what do we need to do?"

* * *

The security team searched the ship, and then, at Nicholen's order, searched it again. Lianndra wasn't in the engine room. She wasn't in the ductwork. She wasn't in a supply closet. She wasn't *anywhere*.

On the bridge, he had Anthony complete a scan of the surrounding solar system while slipping out of geosynchronous orbit and skirting to the other side of the planet. The magnetic field made the scan difficult, but Nicholen was satisfied that no starships were waiting in the area. If she'd mattransed off the anchor ship, that would make their job a whole lot easier: they could shut down all transmissions in and out until the rendezvous time, cutting her off. But if she were hiding inside somewhere— but *where?*—she had physical access to the computer systems.

He slept restlessly, wishing he could distract himself with Xaviara. But they'd made a decision and he would stick to it.

By the morning, his team still hadn't found her. "Keep looking," he ordered. It almost seemed pointless to continue, but they had to do *something*. In the absence of the woman herself, he had to trust that Piotr and Xaviara would be able to stop whatever she was planning.

The time for the rendezvous approached.

Nicholen opened his link. "Are you ready?" he asked Xaviara and Piotr.

"Ready," came her voice.

"And you?" he asked Anthony.

"Yes, sir."

Anthony's fingers were deft across the controls, and information scrolled across the small data screen above his hands. He punched the button for the display, and the wild planet popped onto the wall at the front. It shone verdant and glittering. The planet was gorgeous. What must it have looked like a thousand years ago before the terraforming? A dry dust bowl, perhaps, or an ocean planet with still, icy water.

"Breaking orbit," said Anthony.

Breathtaking and lush, the planet filled the wallscreen as they descended.

"Searching for communication signature," said Samantha. "Nothing yet."

Camlan and Manda have to be at to the pickup location. If they weren't, all this worry about Lianndra would be moot. But both were resourceful, which he knew from his background check on Manda and his long history with the *trincaar.*

"Descending into the mesosphere," said Anthony.

The planet loomed below, the colors resolving into more subtle shades: a forest green section in the top left, a milder green in the bottom left, and the blue of the ocean with cloud cover in the bottom right.

Nicholen realized he was gripping the console in front of himself, and he relaxed. *I fucking hate being along for the ride.*

"Still nothing," said Samantha. "I'm sure we'll have them soon, though."

Chapter 18

Xaviara and Piotr sat side-by-side in his bunk. She was uncomfortable being in his personal space, especially given their long-time rivalry, but she shoved it aside for the sake of the mission. Piotr didn't look much happier about her being there. He'd stuffed an armload of dirty clothes into the laundry chute to clear a seat on the second, tiny stool next to his computer. She sat gingerly on the edge.

As he opened up his display, he promised, "No more naked asses."

His smile cut the tension, and she laughed.

"I'm logged into the mainframe as an administrator profile I created myself," he said. "There's nothing I can do to prevent whatever Lianndra is doing before she does it because I don't know what she's going to try. I've re-purposed a daemon that should be sophisticated enough to detect her, and I can unleash another one to reverse her commands."

The ship's hum changed—a slight increase in volume, although barely noticeable if Xaviara had been going about her daily routine. They must be beginning their descent. Piotr would need to act fast.

"Are you using the ship's daemons?"

"Of course not. They're not specialized enough for that. I have about a dozen I always put into circulation on whatever ship or station I'm on."

Xaviara blinked. "Why would you do that?"

"It's one of those things members of Incongruous always do. Anyway, I like to know things." His fingers were flying across the projected keyboard, and black text scrolled over the display. She caught a few familiar lines, but most were far beyond her knowledge. This wasn't something they would have learned about in her classes.

"Did you know Lianndra was sabotaging the mission?"

He shook his head. "It wasn't something I was looking out for. My daemons are more social in nature."

Does he know about Nicholen and my relationship?

"Social how?"

"I won't tell anyone." His voice was quiet.

She gasped. "You didn't watch us—"

"*No.* Hetero relationships aren't my thing, in the first case, and in the second, I'm a gossip, not a perv."

She forced a chuckle. "But you knew that we... ?"

"When it was heading that way, I shut down the feed. Although I can't say I wasn't curious about his..." He gave her a sidelong glance and lifted an eyebrow.

"Piotr!"

"Tell me it's at least impressive?"

She made a strangled sort of noise, one part incredulity and one part amusement, but she couldn't keep from grinning. He was actually quite funny now that she was getting to know him. And the reminder of what had gone on between herself and Nicholen made a delicious warmth flood between her legs.

"Anyway, I haven't been spying on people any more than a few seconds this trip." His expression soured. "That's why I didn't know about Lianndra's treachery. Although she was probably smart enough to keep it hidden from the feeds. If she had to talk to someone, she would have shut down the audvid. I'm getting a little complacent lately. Nothing new ever happens, just secret relationships and run-of-the-mill kinks. The most interesting thing lately is that people download audvids off the neural net, store them to their links, and watch them in their bunks. It's really quite boring."

"Do I want to know?"

"Not really, but it's mostly just clown porn."

She wasn't sure if he was serious or not, but she laughed anyway.

The ship's hum grew stronger again. They would now be settling into a geosynchronous orbit in the mesosphere near to the pickup location.

"If you're such a brilliant hacker, why did you decide on the ambassador track instead of joining one of those high-paying security firms?" There was a lot more money in the private sector than in diplomacy. A *lot* more.

He was typing away, swiping and looking through three screens at once. She thought he might not answer, but then he said, "Because of my brother."

Startled, she folded her hands in her lap.

"I was young when he was killed. He was fifteen years older than me. I wanted to do something to prevent it from ever happening to someone else's brother, and diplomacy seemed the way to go."

"You're not angry at the kadyyza?"

He punched a couple more buttons. "I was for a long time. But I'm not anymore. Deciding to apply for this job was the final step in healing."

She felt a little guilty for being such a thorn in his side—although he had, when all was said and done, started it.

He pointed to something on the screen. "Here. My daemon found something."

"What is it?"

"I need a moment." He typed away as lines of information flew across the screen. It was dizzying, and Xaviara could make neither heads nor tails of it.

"Uh-oh," he said. "They've made contact with Camlan and Manda. They're about to start the matter transmission. But..."

"But what?" Xaviara leaned forward.

"Found it! Lianndra has inserted a virus into the system that'll scramble their signal. On the bridge, they won't know anything is wrong. We'll pick them up, but they'll never materialize."

Xaviara's heart raced. That would mean she'd never see Manda again. Her friend would just vanish. "Can you stop it?"

"I'll try, but the best way to stop Lianndra is at the point of location."

"But we don't know where she is."

"I do now."

"You found her?"

"Yep." He looked grim. "She's in her bunk."

How was that possible? Realization struck her. "The GK must have someone on Nicholen's security team!"

"Yes. We don't have a moment to lose."

Xaviara ran out the door.

* * *

The sound of the comm beeping cut through the low hum of the bridge.

"It's them!" exclaimed Nicholen. *Thank the forebears. I never thought I'd be so grateful to hear that sound in all my life.*

"Lead ship, this is anchor ship KH-159," responded Samantha. "We read your distress call. Stand by for extraction. Matter transmission initiation protocol commencing."

"I'm going to the mattrans room." Nicholen leapt to his feet and hurried out of the bridge. "You've got this under control?"

"Yes," answered Samantha as the door slid shut on Nicholen.

He ran down the hallway, loping into long strides. *I'm going to see that fucking asshole soon.* Now that Camlan was about to be rescued, Nicholen was furious with him. *Making me take his place as* trincaar. *It should have been me down there.*

He, Camlan, and the *trincaarit* were going to have a good, long discussion after this. There might be shouting. *No, no "might" about it. There will definitely be shouting.*

Hurrying through the door of the mattrans room, Nicholen prepared to throw his arms around his liege and long-time friend. Instead, human Engineering Officer Hazel stood behind the tri-d control bank, hands poised in the air. The landing pad was devoid of anyone.

"Where are they?" he demanded.

"I'm waiting for them to get into position," responded the older woman.

"I thought they *were* in position."

Her eyes snapped to his. She might be a junior staff member—someone who'd joined the Coalition in her late fifties, if he remembered her dossier correctly—but she was still three decades his senior. He'd seen that look on his own Nana's face before. He was about to get a tongue lashing, even though she had to know he was supposedly a prince.

"My apologies," he hurried out the words. "Please continue with your duties."

She sniffed and turned back to the display. "We're on open comm to the bridge. Samantha has instructed them to seek higher ground. We're unable to cut through the magnetic field to extract them at their current altitude."

"*Fuck.*" At Hazel's look, Nicholen wished he'd chosen a less translatable swear.

Nicholen's link beeped with Xaviara's chime, and he pressed behind his ear. "Go ahead."

"We found Lianndra!" *Thank the forebears.* "She's in her room. One of your security team must have sneaked her back in."

"*Moklonish jixxis!*" he swore. This was not good at all. He turned toward the door, ready to storm through the ship and throw every one of his personnel into the brig. Who could it be? Eemon? Kalliph? It couldn't possibly be Thoxxin, his second-in-command, could it?

But Xaviara wasn't done. "She's messing about with the mattrans. She's inserted a virus into the system that will allow the beam to initiate, but they'll never make it to the ship. She'll scatter their molecules across the ocean instead, and we'll never be able to get them back."

Nicholen's heart nearly stopped beating. "Are you able to stop it?"

"Piotr's trying, but he says she was given advanced training by the *Geshhina Kadyyza*. Her daemons are evading his."

"Is he going to be successful?"

"I don't know, but I'm at her bunk right now."

"What? It's too dangerous!"

"I'm about to break in with a physical chipset. I have to insert it into her bank, and it'll halt her virus. It's the only way for sure to stop her. You have to hold off the mattrans until you get the all clear from me."

"Wait for me, Xaviara!"

But her link beeped to sever the connection.

Before he ran out the door, he addressed Hazel. "You have to wait. There's a virus that will disrupt the mat-trans."

Hazel nodded. Samantha's voice came over the comm. "We have another problem. They're still not high enough, and indigenous life forms on the planet are becoming aggressive. We need to get them out as soon as possible."

"*Fuck!*" shouted Nicholen, and this time he didn't feel guilty from Hazel's look of disapproval.

"They're still climbing," she said, "but they're only within the 95% safety range. Safety procedures won't let me extract them until 99.95%."

He considered overriding the protocols, but the safety ranges existed for a reason. "Keep tabs on them. The second the levels are within tolerance, *be ready to get them the fuck out of there.*"

Without waiting for acknowledgment, he raced out the door toward the kadyyza quarters.

Chapter 19

Xaviara wiped the palm of her hand on her uniform. She practiced hand-to-hand combat on a regular weekly rotation, but she'd never *actually* had to use it before. If Lianndra was knowledgeable about viral warfare, wouldn't they also have trained her in kadyyza martial arts?

Xaviara waved Piotr's illicit security device near the door. He'd said it was the latest technology out of the fifth sector from a race of aliens the humans had secured relations with recently. Things were still rocky between them and the kadyyza, so it was unlikely Lianndra had any method of counteracting the override.

The door beeped angrily. The light blinked red—*Is this going to work?*—and then glowed green.

Clutching the chipset in one hand, Xaviara slammed her hand into the door open button.

"What the..." Lianndra jumped up from her display, spewing a string of kadyyza swears the translator failed to understand. On the wall beyond her head was the bank of nodes Xaviara needed.

"In the name of the Sol Alliance Coalition, I order you to stop. I'm placing you under diplomatic arrest. Come with me to the brig immediately." Xaviara's voice rang out strong and true.

Lianndra's face twisted in rage as she backed against the wall. "You can't stop me. You're way too late for that. The *trincaar* is going to die."

She's stalling. Any minute, Camlan and Manda would be beamed off the planet. Xaviara couldn't play it cool here. She had to get the chipset inserted. "Get out of my way!" She leaped forward, reaching for the wall.

Lianndra kicked out, hitting Xaviara in the stomach and reeling her backward.

"Ugh!" came the involuntarily outrush of air from her lungs as she slammed in the wall of the tiny bunk. Xaviara sucked in a breath, seeing red and fighting to push herself forward. "You're not going to win."

Lianndra's purple skin glowed in the dim light of her bunk. Information scrolled past on the display. "You don't know anything about what I'm doing. I *am* going to succeed."

Xaviara slid the chipset into her uniform's pocket. Leaping forward again, she was ready this time. When Lianndra kicked out, she blocked downward.

Holy OW. She'd only once had a partner this rough, and she'd sworn not to spar with him again. Maybe that was a poor decision—she definitely wasn't ready for the pain of real combat. Her forearm smarted with the force of the blow.

Lifting her other arm, she attempted a downward swing, sloppy and inept, but it was only a ruse. Lianndra blocked it, allowing Xaviara the opportunity to punch her right in the solar plexus.

Lianndra dropped like a rock.

Xaviara plunged her hand into the pocket and yanked out the chipset. Before she could insert it, Lianndra grabbed her by the ankle and twisted.

Falling, Xaviara lost hold of the chipset. It went spinning onto the desk.

Lianndra climbed on top of her, lilac lips lifted into a sneer. She wrapped her hands around Xaviara's neck and squeezed. "Let me guess. Nicholen has finally decided to put his cock to use."

The room started to fade.

No way she's going to win!

Xaviara slammed her arms up into Lianndra's as hard as she could. Something popped as Lianndra's arms came loose, and Lianndra let out a screaming wail. "My fucking arm! You broke my fucking—"

Xaviara kicked her off, leapt to her feet, grabbed the chipset, and slammed it into the bank.

"*Hell yes!*" came Piotr's voice in her link. Through the haze of pain and adrenaline, Xaviara wondered how he'd linked the two of them without her knowledge.

A voice came from the door. "Verrytto Lianndra, you are under arrest by the Imdali Royal Guard." It was

Nicholen's second-in-command Thoxxin. "You will be sentenced and tried by the Royal Court." He stepped inside, hauling a wailing Lianndra to her feet. "You have the right to representation after your initial interrogation. You have the right to withhold statement, but..."

As the guard continued to read Lianndra her rights, Xaviara heaved a giant breath. "Piotr, is it safe?"

"One sec," he said. "Just another... moment... Yes! Go!"

She pressed the link behind her ear. "Open comm to Nicholen: Commence matter transmission. The virus has been neutralized. Get them off that horrible planet!"

* * *

Nicholen was halfway to Lianndra's bunk when Xaviara's voice came through. "What happened?"

"Your guard is here. Thoxxin, I think?" she said. "He's arresting her."

Thoxxin's voice sounded distant, along with the Lianndra's wails. "I have Eemon already in the brig, sir. He was aiding and abetting her."

Relief flooded through him. Nicholen turned around to sprint back the direction he came. Bursting into the mat-trans room, he shouted, "Go, Hazel, go!"

Hazel swiped a hand left, then right, then pinched together in the gesture to initiate the transmission. "They're still not high enough. There's still a chance we won't get them out of there."

"*What?*"

"I can't yet. They're still climbing." She flicked a finger and a pixelated image of Camlan and Manda appeared in the air. The white, shimmering dots hung between them. The two were strapped into climbing gear and making their way up thick vines with carabiners. "She's almost there, but it'll take him a few minutes longer."

"What the *hell* is that?" Nicholen said.

A gigantic tentacle was reaching up through the air toward the real *trincaar.*

"Must be the indigenous life form Samantha was talking about." Hazel's hands stayed poised in the air. "They lost their communication device moments ago."

"How?"

"Slipped out of Camlan's hands."

Fucking idiot. But he couldn't fault the man, who was apparently hanging over a cavern with some sort of *creature* after them. Nicholen pressed his fingernails into the palm of his hand. The tentacle wavered in the air, still some meters from the two.

"She's almost there," said Hazel. "99.27%. She's almost—"

"Safety override to 99.25% authorized by *Trincaar* Valkkh Camlan," shouted Nicholen.

The ship beeped confirmation, and Hazel pinched her fingers together. *They better have truly neutralized that fucking virus.* Manda's dots faded, and he stared at the landing pad. *Just another moment... just another moment...* As Manda disappeared from the display completely, she materialized on the pad, arm outstretched.

"Oof!" she grunted as she fell half a meter onto the floor.

"Sorry, ma'am, had to make sure you would end up above the pad."

She leapt to her feet. "We have to extract Camlan!"

Nicholen stepped forward. "I've lowered the safety protocols to—"

"No time to wait for safety protocols! There's something attacking him. You have to get him out of there!"

Hazel said, "He's dropping."

Nicholen whirled.

"Dropping?" shouted Manda. "Not dropping, just... lowering. There's a *thing* in the canyon behind him. It's got hold of him!"

The pixelated image showed the tentacle wrapped around his leg. *Forebears, what the fuck do I do?* Camlan seemed to be holding a knife, his leg was extended downward, and he was struggling to reach it.

"He's losing centimeters of altitude," Hazel's voice was calm. "98.5% safety... 98.4% safety..."

"He'll make it," said Nicholen. Wouldn't he? "Just wait, we can't—"

"*Just pull him out of there!* Safety override to 95% authorized by Lead Manda Aurellia!"

The computer beeped to acknowledge her command, and Nicholen leapt toward the controls before Hazel could react. He pinched his fingers together himself, relieved he was finally *doing* something.

On the display, Camlan lunged downward, his outline visibly struggling as he hacked at the creature. With one last stab, his vine rocketed upward—he'd hacked off the tentacle, and the momentum was carrying him upward.

At the apex, the mattrans took hold. And then, inside the room, Camlan was falling to the floor, a brown tentacle wrapped around his leg, dripping green slime and smelling like days-old rotten fruit.

"Holy fuck, old friend." Nicholen pressed a hand to his nose. "That *reeks*."

"So glad to be home," moaned Camlan from the floor.

Manda ran over, threw her arms around him, and pressed her mouth to his in a passionate kiss that impressed even Nicholen.

Chapter 20

The next eight hours were a whirlwind of activity. Camlan, Gloria, and Manda had to be debriefed, and Lianndra and Eemon questioned. The real *trincaar* decided it was time to tell the entire ship their true identities and lift whatever psy-ability he had used to keep it a secret; closed door meetings and apologies commenced, with Nicholen sitting uncomfortably by his side. He had no time to even acknowledge Xaviara beyond a wink and a smile, and anyway, Manda put her aide to work almost immediately upon stepping foot out of the mat-trans room.

Lianndra was her typical stubborn self, refusing to give any useful information in the initial interview, but Nicholen was much less exasperated with her than he'd been for years. He was finally vindicated. He'd proved she was up to no good. Although it saddened him on Camlan's behalf, the *trincaar*'s big heart and forgiving nature had almost cost him his life. Nicholen didn't go easy on the woman.

"Tell me," he stood in front of the cell with his arms crossed and his feet shoulder-width apart, "why did you do it?"

"Do what?" she answered sweetly.

"Don't give me that shit, Lianndra. We caught you red-handed."

Her lips pressed into a thin line.

I'm getting a confession out of her, one way or another. "You think you're clever, but I've been onto you since the beginning, haven't I?"

She looked to be struggling not to answer, but she finally responded, "Yeah, but *you* didn't catch me. Your little lover did, huh?"

Nicholen replayed the past few days' events in his head. They'd both figured it out at the same time. But— "It doesn't matter. In the end, you got caught. You GK are all the same. Too blinded by your own ideals to pull something like this off."

"Oh, really?" She smirked up at him.

Willex's death hung in the air between them. He scowled. "You were too young when that happened, my dear. You had nothing to do with it."

"I have no idea what you're talking about."

"Oh, you do. You definitely do. What made you run to the GK anyway? I didn't think you were a supremacist."

"I wasn't," she said.

"Until?"

She didn't answer.

"I'll just have to assume that you're easily susceptible to brainwashing."

That got her. "It doesn't take brainwashing to realize that Camlan's too dumb to be *trincaarit*!"

"What? He is not!" Nicholen reined in his temper. "He'll make a fine *trincaarit*."

She leaned forward, face twisted in rage. "First of all, he wouldn't listen to what I had to say. If I were to be his wife, we needed to rule equally."

"That's true, but he had to have a reason for not listening."

"He said my ideas weren't 'in line with the forebears' teachings.' Like we should listen to some crackly old audvids over someone in the here and now! A lot of it's not relevant anymore. The *Geshhina Kadyyza* get that. We needed to remove the *trincaar* to make way for a new order."

"You're rambling." Even though he now had the upper hand, he couldn't help but needle this woman who had pissed him off for so long.

"I'm not— Fine." She sat back, dropping her eyes to her pant leg again. "Anyway. The other reason was that when I cheated on him, he forgave me. I was mad at him for that. A *trincaarit* should be ruthless. Have no mercy. We can't have a ruler who's unwilling to do what it takes."

Nicholen shook his head. "You're sad, Lianndra, and your reasoning is absurd. I feel no pity for you. And the courts will make sure you get what you deserve."

"We'll see about that," she muttered, but the threat was empty, and her look of resignation told him she knew it.

Nicholen turned on his heel and marched out of the brig.

Three hours later, they were docking at the Imdali Intersolar Space Station. Waiting on the landing pad was none other than the *trincaarit*, Travid Valkkh, surrounded by attendees and with his wife at his shoulder. *Now there's a woman who's the equal of her mate.* Lianndra truly didn't understand it. A *trin* was much more than a ruler. She was a diplomat, a hub of information, and the backbone of the royal family. Ophenia Valkkh was all that and more, a true match for her man.

It made his thoughts drift to Xaviara.

"Camlan, glad to see you're safe." Travid embraced his son in what looked to be a rib-cracking hug. Nicholen had given Travid's Captain a short debrief via link while they were en route.

Travid, like Nicholen's long-time friend, had a large heart. He could be cold and calculating when he wanted to, but the desire for warmth and love was bred into the royal line by the forebears. Travid embodied all those characteristics, and it made him a fair and capable ruler over the kadyyza.

"Nicholen," said Travid, "thank you for keeping my son safe."

Nicholen inclined his head deeply toward the *trincaarit*, who laughed and pulled him into an embrace. *Yep, rib-cracking.* As soon as the large man let him go, Nicholen sucked in a quiet breath.

"The two of you, come with me," said Travid. "We need to have a discussion about what went on."

Camlan caught Nicholen's eye. His usual goofy demeanor was replaced by something serious. Despite his calm resolution, Nicholen's stomach dropped. Would he be blamed for the crash and near fatal extraction? *I should have protested the swap more. I should never have agreed to this. What was I thinking? I should have...*

Travid's deep indigo cape whirled behind him as he headed toward a private meeting room off the docking bay. He stopped to kiss Ophenia, who muttered something that sounded like, "Don't go too hard on him," in his ear.

Once they were alone, Nicholen steeled himself for a tongue lashing.

"Nicholen, my boy, I want to commend you on an excellent rescue mission and on uncovering one of the key rogue operatives for our biggest terrorist organization," said Travid. "You've grown into a fine Captain of the *Trincaar's* Royal Guard, and I'm certain we've chosen well for the future. You'll make an excellent Captain of the *Trincaarit's* Guard when Camlan takes over from me. I'm recommending you for a Tri-Color Medal and a fifteen percent raise."

Nicholen's mouth dropped open.

"Furthermore, I understand you've found a girlfriend."

Nicholen's stomach dropped. *Now* would there be a reprimand? He could have jeopardized the treaty. "I can explain."

Travid shook his head. "She's cute, son. I've been briefed on her background, and I approve. She makes an excellent match for you. I hope you can make it work." He guffawed. "And here Camlan and I thought you'd never pick a mate."

Camlan, who had looked somewhat stunned up to this point, laughed along with his father.

"The two of you talk about me?" asked Nicholen weakly.

That only made them laugh harder.

"I'm not to be reprimanded, then?" He had to ask.

"The rules are there to ensure nothing untoward happens during the negotiations. I think we can cite extenuating circumstances. You're being granted special dispensation. Just don't try to influence the terms of the accord." Travid's look was stern.

"Why would I... ?" Oh, it was a joke. "I won't, sir."

"That's all I had to say to you." Travid clapped him on the back of the shoulder. "Camlan and I have other things to discuss. Go to her. Make her as happy as she makes you."

"What do you mean?"

"You're glowing," said Camlan. "And you're much less uptight than usual."

Nicholen wanted to punch his friend in the arm, but he restrained himself in front of the *trincaarit*. "Oh, like you're one to talk. I saw that kiss in the mattrans room."

Camlan's blush said it all.

* * *

Xaviara was in her opulent guest suite when the door chime sounded. Heart in her throat, she leapt up. *Don't seem too eager. It might not even be him.*

Manda had her running in circles, and Xaviara was only now relaxing in quarters four times the size of the ones on Sol Alliance Space Station 47. It could be her boss again, finding some chore to do, a spreadsheet to build, an analysis to run, or an impromptu meeting to attend.

The longest break Xaviara had taken that day was to check her birth control nano-bots: still in place and running at peak capacity. The act of opening her medical interface in her link made her face heat. She had no idea if they were necessary with an alien of another species, but she wanted to be ready.

So when the door chimed, she couldn't keep the excitement from her voice when she said, "Come in!"

Nicholen stepped inside, and the door slid shut behind him. Without the cape and in the uniform of the Captain of the Guard, he made a sexy, imposing figure. Xaviara allowed herself the indulgence of running her eyes across his defined pecs and down his torso, where she knew the washboard abs that awaited.

In two strides, he was across the room, kissing her. Unrestrained this time by the stresses of finding a saboteur, she threw a leg around his waist to find him hard already. Desire surged inside her, and she clenched her inner muscles as she ran a hand through his hair. His tongue found hers and their lust battled.

He pulled away, leaving her breathless. "How are the negotiations?"

"Everything is going smoothly. It looks like the space-way is happening sooner than we thought." Xaviara ran a hand down his chest, reconfirming the rock hard muscles underneath. *This man is breathtaking.* She felt buzzing, alive—nervous and excited at the same time.

Without another word, he kissed her again and then lifted her other leg to pick her up. Carefully, still kissing her, he walked to the bed and laid her down. He gathered her long hair and pulled it to the side to nuzzle her neck.

"There's something else," said Xaviara.

He paused his exploration at her ear, nibbled it once, and whispered, "Tell me."

She shivered. "Manda has requested being stationed with the ambassadorial team here in Imdali. Gloria has granted her request. She asked me if I wanted to come with. I've been thinking about it since this afternoon."

He pulled back. "What are you going to tell her?"

She let a mischievous grin spread across her face. "It depends on how good the rest of the payback is."

He licked his lips. "Then I'd better get to work."

Nicholen ran his hands down her body. He stopped to massage her breasts and then pulled her shirt up over her head. Quickly, he unfastened her bra and tossed it to the side. Once she was free of the garments, he nuzzled his way down to her uniform pants and hooked a finger in each side. "You are gorgeous."

Warmth flooded her. As he pulled down her pants to reveal pink cotton panties, she thought about all that had happened in such a short amount of time. Three days ago, she was bemoaning her prospects, and today, she'd found a well-traveled, sexy captain of a guard who was running his hands across her body like he'd found a prize jewel.

Nicholen leaned back to lift his shirt over his head. His blue skin made her shiver—so exotic, so sexy, so gorgeous. His pants were off in another instant, and his manhood sprang free of his boxers.

"Are you sure?" he asked.

"More than sure." The wetness in her panties was testament to her words.

Gently, he pulled them down, suckling at the base of her thigh, teasing and tormenting her until she moaned. He spread her lips, looking down at her. "Pink is a good color." He flicked a tongue over her bundle of nerves and then over it again.

"I want you inside me," she gasped.

"Happy to oblige." He pulled her panties off the rest of the way and climbed onto the bed. Positioning himself at her entrance, he smiled down at her. But then his look melted.

"What's wrong?"

"You're going to tell them yes, aren't you?" His voice was anxious.

She smiled. "Yes, of course. Your psy-sense hasn't told you that?"

"Well... I..."

His hesitance was cute, and she found it even more endearing with the feel of his manhood against her. She reached down to caress his hard length, swirling it around her entrance. "I love that I can get you flustered." One hand crept to his ass, and the other held him in position.

With a gentle tug, she pulled him inside her, gasping as he filled her to the brim.

"Fuck," he groaned. "You feel so good."

Relaxing her grip, she let him pull out and push back in. The rhythm built up, so perfect, so right. She ran a hand over his face as he thrust inside her, and then she kissed his lips, tasting him and feeling him and wanting more, more...

"*More*," she moaned.

He was happy to oblige, increasing his rhythm and running his hands across her breasts. "You are my match, my little *viaar*," he whispered in her ear. "I'm glad you're staying here."

"Me, too," she gasped, letting the pleasure build inside her.

She was tensing, writhing, so close, so close... With her cry, the orgasm crashed over her, and she was moaning, and he was moaning, and they were clutching each other and crying out.

As he relaxed and lowered himself gently onto her in the wake of their lovemaking, she said, "I'm so glad I found you."

"And I'm glad I found you," he answered.

Free Short Story!

I f you like my work and want to be notified when I'm releasing something new, sign up for my newsletter at:

http://ariel-jade.com/free-stuff/

As a bonus, you'll receive an electronic copy of my erotic romance short story "The Duke's Plaything."

He has a magical secret. She's agreed to keep it.

About the Author

Ariel Jade loves romance—the hotter, the better. She also loves sci-fi—the more futuristic, the better. Mashing the two together comes naturally. Fans of Anna Hackett—or anyone who thinks Nalini Singh should write in a Star Trek-ish universe—will love her thrilling, sizzling sci-fi romance.

Find out more about her works at www.ariel-jade.com.

www.ingramcontent.com/pod-product-compliance
Lightning Source LLC
Jersburg PA
J21047130626
2CB00005B/2055